GW00690537

WRITERS
REIGN

A collection of short stories, poems and puzzles.

Published in 2017 by the Thames Valley Writers' Circle.

Cover design by Emma Rose Bell.

ISBN 978-0-9955984-0-9

Printed by Direct-POD
www.direct-pod.com

The Thames Valley Writers' Circle is a group of writers of mixed ability, with ages ranging from 18 to 90. Some of us have had work published, while others prefer to write for their own pleasure or even as therapy.

We are not a tutored group. Our aim is to improve our writing ability by listening to the work of others, reading our own work and getting feedback through helpful and constructive criticism.

If you are interested in writing, why not join us? The Circle meets every Tuesday evening between 7.30 and 9.30 pm at St Joseph's Church Hall, Berkshire Drive, Tilehurst RG31 5JJ.

There are breaks for Christmas, Easter and a longer break in August.

Visit our website: www.thamesvalleywriterscircle.org

Some of the short stories in this anthology were entries in two of our regular internal competitions.

Miscellaneous Haiku and short poems have been added (anonymously) purely to fill up the empty spaces.

There are also a few puzzles to exercise the little grey cells.

We hope you enjoy our anthology.

CONTENTS

The Erase Button

I don't know if this old tape recorder will still record. In a way I hope it doesn't, but it would be nice to get some stuff off my chest. Then I'll erase the tape before anyone finds it, if I can free the seized erase button.

As Christmas is coming I'll start there. Some people say they don't like Christmas, it's all work and hassle. Me, I love it because once those mad few days of angst, family tensions, and rows are over, the rest of the year seems such a breeze. Have you noticed how families drive for miles around the country on Christmas morning to meet up in the home of the one who's drawn the shortest straw? It's our equivalent of the African wildebeest migration. Of course wildebeest only have to face flooded rivers and crocodiles, which is no risk at all compared to Brussels sprouts. Many of those that complain about Christmas just grit their teeth and get on with it because what we Brits love most is self inflicted wounds: like going to the coast on rainy Bank holidays, living with crooked teeth, and Brexit. We love to suffer, and Christmas is our Mecca; whoops, can I say that these days?

This year I'll be going to Charlie and Beryl's again, they have such rotten luck in the short straw department. And poor old Charlie, why he married my Beryl I'll never know. Oh dear, I really hope later on I can free that erase button.

I shouldn't say this but the highlight of last year's Christmas was when Charlie carried a brandy soaked flaming Christmas pudding in to the dining room from the kitchen. Well, he'd obviously had a snifter or two because his brandy dribbled mat of badger road-kill that he calls a beard suddenly whooshed up. He dropped the flaming pudding and began frantically beating at the badger. Beryl was screaming, "Roll on the floor Charlie, smother the flames". He dropped to the floor and was rolling and writhing when whoosh the nylon carpet went up with him. My other two daughters and their husbands and all the kids were cheering wildly, assuming it was another of Charlie's Christmas pranks. I could see it was serious but my fits of laughter became uncontrollable; it took two days to dry my chair out. Beryl phoned me last week, apparently we're having cheese cake this year. I didn't say anything but I ask you, what sort of Christmas is that?

Beryl has taken to phoning me quite regularly lately and usually ends our chat with something along the lines of, "Where exactly do you keep the deeds of the house Mum". I think it's the bad cough I've had for months that's prompting the questioning. And heaven knows why she keeps telling

1

me I don't need the heating on until there's ice on the insides of the windows.

Beryl, Mavis and Marjorie are my three girls. They're all in their fifties now. Reg and I thought it would be nice to have three girls, growing up together; playing with their dolls and prams, party frocks and pretend tea parties. Fought like pit-bulls they did, we could have sold tickets. It's not surprising everyone in the village called them the Bitches of Eastwick. They're all married. Or I should say they're all married again, and again. How I'm expected to remember their husband's names is beyond me. Even Marjorie, who is on husband number five, gets confused. Last year during the Christmas fire she shouted at her husband, "Bill, don't just stand there laughing, fetch some water". That created shocked looks around the table because Bill was actually husband number one. She then proceeded to yell her way though the list, "Graham, Joe, Peter," and eventually "Robert, fetch some water". I don't think it's fair on the kids.

Although I like Christmas it does have a down side. Present giving. And just as bad in my view, present receiving. Convoys of container ships set sail from China from July onwards, headed our way and loaded with tat. Why we scrapped our submarine fleet is a mystery to me. At least if the containers were lost at sea it would save hours of pointless wrapping, sellotaping (if you can find the end) and label writing. Instead we have clogged ports, stuffed warehouses and jammed motorways as shiny plastic trinkets and fake perfume make the fateful journey to that heap beneath the Christmas tree. And who said we Brits are gullible? Actually quite a few people have said that, but as they're all foreigners they obviously don't count.

I've been told to go online to do my Christmas shopping. Are they kidding. I can scarcely operate this old tape recorder so how am I supposed to grapple with that sort of technology. Besides, our Sinclair Spectrum is still in its box in the loft and I'm not clambering up there just to get into the 21st century.

The art of present giving and receiving lies of course in the skill of recycling. And let me tell you, this sort of recycling predates the council's green, grey, red, pink, tangerine, and lilac coloured wheelie bins that take up most of my back garden. I have kept notes for years of who gave me which present, and the year I gave it back to them. I don't do a simple, "Oh if that's all you think of me you can have it back next year". Oh no, I hang fire for a few years, the not knowing makes them anxious. There's a box of pomegranate and garlic scented bath salts that's been back and forth for seven years to my certain knowledge. To break the chain I'm giving it to Ray this year, that's Mavis's husband (number four, if you're wondering).

The grandchildren make me hand crafted presents. They're all rubbish of course but I can see their point. Why spend money on something thoughtful for grandma when they can knock something out from the cardboard tube of a toilet roll. I blame Blue Peter.

I won't decorate the house this year. I don't know why I mentioned that, I haven't put decorations up for twelve years so I'm hardly likely to start now. Besides, with that new street light the council has put outside the house that flickers all night what do I need more for? I bet that came from China.

"What are you bringing this year Mum"? That was Beryl phoning again.

"Just myself darling, what could be nicer" is what I said, in my head. "What would you like me to bring" is what I actually said.

"Well, Charlie thought some wine would be a good idea" she said.

"Fine" I told her, "I'll do that".

"Lovely" she replied, "let's say six red and six white".

It's a good job I was sitting down. After I'd recovered I got a bus into town and went to the Poundshop where I found a Tibetan red and a North Korean white. I bought two bottles of each, I couldn't carry any more. I shall go back soon to get the others. To be honest, I didn't think a pound a bottle was too extravagant.

Mavis has told me that on Christmas morning Ray will come and pick me up. I don't like to sound ungrateful but an eighty two year old wedged into the sidecar of a motorbike is not very dignified, but before I could find the right words to refuse she'd said, "So that's agreed then", and put the phone down.

There's only two weeks to go. The excitement is not mounting. I've wrapped the presents. And that's another thing that lot of mine don't appreciate, how much time I put into ironing out the wrinkles in last years wrapping paper, and snowing out the writing on the tags. It seems to take longer as the paper ages and wrinkles more, and the snowing gets thicker.

So I'll say goodbye now. It's been most therapeutic getting that off my chest and all I need to do is free that erase button before my darling children find this tape. Oh, I can hear the phone ringing. I'll do the erase later, but I am getting so forgetful lately.

by Les Williams

The Goddess Juliet

"We'll shortly be landing at Romeo International Airport. Please fasten your seatbelts and make sure your seat backs are upright."

Out of the window I saw the mountains of New Verona rising sheer, straight from the sea, and appreciated immediately why the island had remained unknown and unvisited for so long. The place was so inhospitable that even its harbour was relatively new. Now it actually boasted its own airport, although it remained one of the most dangerous in the world. I closed my eyes and muttered a silent prayer as rock faces slipped past, seemingly inches from the wing tips.

As soon as we were past the wall of mountains, the plane went into a steep dive before levelling out for landing, and I breathed a sigh as the engine note returned to normal.

"Nervous Father?" the girl next to me said. "Surely God will protect you."

I'd grown used to the hinted sneer of non-Christians and I gave her a Teflon smile. "He protects the soul," I murmured, "not necessarily the body, and old and decrepit though mine is, I'd still like to keep it."

The tannoy pinged. "For those who have never visited New Verona before, you can see the famous statue of Juliet on the left."

The bible is quite clear about idolatry, and for me even the gigantic statue of Jesus that towered over Rio was somewhat offensive, but this was something else again. The monstrosity that suddenly appeared was all the more ghastly to me because it seemed to mock the Holy Madonna. How many hospitals, I wondered, could have been built with the resources that went into its construction? I groaned inwardly at the applause and cries of 'praise be' from the pilgrims on the plane. I was all too aware of those who had seen my dog-collar gauging my reaction and sniggering. As always, I donned my mask of pleasantness while I seethed underneath. Jesus had died for these morons... Uncharitable? So what? I'm getting too old for this.

Perhaps that was why Her Ladyship Archbishop Alice Runcible had sent me on this mission to visit High Priest Tybalt – clearly an assumed name – one of the leaders of this odious little cult. She'd known I'd tell them exactly what I thought. The phenomenon of lovelorn people writing pathetic letters to a fictional character – Juliet letters, they were called – had snowballed into a cult that major religions had to take seriously? It needed putting in its place.

The driver was a chatty enough fellow until I punctured his balloon.

"You don't really believe in this nonsense," I said, as we drove the main highway from the airport to the Temple of Juliet, another over-elaborate construction, that dominated New Verona's skyline.

He didn't speak again, and I caught sight of his jaw working angrily when I looked at his rear-view mirror. Funny how charm and intellect are often skin deep, I thought with a smile. I resorted to gazing out of the window at the passing scenery. I had to yield a certain grudging respect for the industry and the beauty of some of the buildings, but everyone I saw seemed to have the vacant placid smile of the fanatic plastered on their faces.

The self-styled High Patriarch greeted me with a warm smile and the firm handshake of a driven evangelist.

"Welcome Bishop Hatter," he said before leading me to his private audience chamber, which I'd swear was more luxurious than anything the Vatican had to offer. He offered me a glass of sherry. I actually needed a whisky after that flight, but let it go.

"There's no sense in pretending this is going to be an easy meeting," I said bluntly. "Cults such as yours are always rising and falling, and I strongly suspect yours will go the way of Waco. Nevertheless, here we are."

"Indeed." If he was affronted, he didn't show it.

"People are often fooled into ascribing more to something than its worth, and while asking advice from a child in a play might seem foolish, raising that child to the status of a deity, as you have done, seems to many to be irresponsible." I went straight for the jugular.

He shrugged and spread his arms. "People pray to the baby Jesus in the same way," he said. "Why, he even died as she did."

"There's no comparison!" The thought crossed my mind that the Muslims wouldn't put up with such blasphemy. "Juliet is a fictional character, nothing more. It is ridiculous to pretend that the creation of someone's imagination could become some kind of god or goddess."

"Yet here we are," he said, with an irritating smirk. "The wisdom of Juliet has been passed to us by his prophet Shakespeare."

"It was a play. Nothing more!" I said deliberately, as if explaining to a child. "There is no divine wisdom in it."

"Yet people have been seeking it out long before her Church became established. They turned their back on your institutions because they couldn't find the answers they needed there. Perhaps you should accept that it is time we moved on from Christianity."

Worse than I'd thought. "Christianity isn't just a fad that people 'get bored with'!'"

"I agree. But try to think of it as a stage towards human enlightenment."

"The enlightenment of Juliet?" I sneered.

"Perhaps she's just the next stage. We once thought that our ancestors became gods. Then as pagans we thought each aspect of nature was divine, before recognising that there could only be one god, whose nature developed as our understanding grew. Religion has always been amorphous, yet at each stage people have always dedicated themselves heart and soul to whatever they believed in, often creating amazing things in his her or its name. Sneer all you like; you can't take that away from them."

I'd heard enough of these arguments over the years, and they always end up going round in circles or even, in my younger seminary days, coming to blows. I forced myself to relax, and smiled saying that I'd certainly discuss what he'd said with the Archbishop, which was always going to be the outcome of our meeting anyway. He was never going to convert me and I wasn't going to convert him.

He took me on a tour of the temple and it's exhibits, and as we strolled through the gardens where young acolytes were practising their fencing, I asked him what Juliet had to say about the afterlife.

"You should read the play," he said. "She died to be reunited with her love. No heaven or hell. Love is the only thing that transcends death."

I dozed as the plane taxied to the runway for its return journey, remembering the old vicar who had calmed the confusions of my youth. 'You know,' he'd told me, 'that peace and salvation come from true faith. It doesn't matter how powerful the arguments are against it, or even if that faith makes life difficult for you. Believe without question, and you will always be strong.'

He'd been right. When people laughed and insulted me, I didn't have to fight battles I couldn't win, because in the end I could be secure in my faith. That's what led me ultimately to the priesthood.

As the engines wound up for take-off I comforted myself with that faith and felt strong, able to consider Tybalt's words with equanimity. However, it is when one feels strong that one is most vulnerable.

It was true that Juliet had been transformed into something far beyond the tragic child in Shakespeare's play. She had become an icon from which people had undoubtedly found comfort. Their faith gave them strength, and had enabled them to transform New Verona into a Garden of Eden, which was almost a miracle in itself.

The plane accelerated down the runway, and as it leapt into the air my eyes snapped open. There before me was Juliet, her face glowing in the morning sun. The impact of that beauty on me was almost physical. In that moment I realised that despite everything, I'd never truly loved anyone or anything.

The screaming engines forced me into my seat, and as the plane shook in its fight to clear the mountains, I felt parts of my soul fall away. I prayed harder than ever that the wingtips would miss the rock faces so that I'd get the chance to put it together again before I died.

by Nick Telepneff

The Tragedy

By Colin Ferguson

A doorway his stage and a box his bed,
For comfort, its print smudged and pictures blurred.
Yesterday's news makes pillows for his head.
Forgotten man lies on forgotten word.
He rests not far from where the crowds gave praise;
once famous, he now huddles in his rags,
mumbling his memories in strong brew haze;
his fortune held in two brown paper bags.
Then he could strut and be the noble king,
Or tumble as the jester in the play,
But confidence was always laced with gin
And soon made him forget what he should say.
Now as the wandering fool his role is cast.
It is his saddest and will be his last.

No Love Lost

John hesitated before lifting the latch. He was tired and needed to rest, but there was no chance of that in this house.

He shook his head and opened the door to be greeted by a smoke filled room, and Mary, his wife, hammering on their son's locked door.

"Come out at once. I need the wood chopped. If you don't come out I'll get an axe and chop this door down."

There was no response. There never was.

While he waited for the assault to be over, he opened the front door fully and watched the smoke escaping into the street. Then he rearranged the fire, added another log, and waited for it to settle.

The fire spat at him with the same force as his wife's words.

It would be nice if now and again he could come home to a quiet house.

Mary entered the room carrying a mug of ale and slammed it down on the table splashing it all over his best clothes. Anger was beginning to take hold of him.

"It's all your fault." Her words pierced him.

"What's all my fault now?"

"It was a son I wanted and what did you give me - a pale shadow of a youth, who never lifts a finger to help me. He hides in his room scratching away at his letters, as if he was somebody important who didn't need to find a job."

"Shut up woman, just leave him alone. I've had enough of your lip."

Not for the first time he wondered how an educated man like himself could be so coarse when he was talking to his wife.

"It's always your fault and you know it." Her words entered him like daggers.

This was the last straw. He fired back at her.

"How can that be. You told me he wasn't mine years ago. Even you can't have it both ways. Whatever the truth is, he is still my son. If it hadn't been for him, I would have divorced you long ago." He really had lost it completely and he would be made to regret it.

She walked over to the spit and turned it thoughtfully. John wondered if she was planning her next onslaught or perhaps wishing that she had never married him.

She spun round, shaking her ladle at him. "He just sits in that cupboard of a room, writing well into the night. He reads Latin and Greek yet he can't even spell his own name."

"Calm down. He can hear every word you say." He was beginning to feel that he was losing the battle once again. He waited in silence for her to continue.

"He got through nineteen candles last week. Where am I going to get the money for those? At this rate I will have to go on the streets."

"I wish you would - then all of us would get some peace." John shouted but she wasn't even listening. He might as well not have been there. Maybe if he didn't ever answer her she would get fed up with nagging him. After all, if she wasn't upsetting him, what would be the point? If he laughed or smiled that might work but ...

She laid into him again "He isn't even interested in girls. Takes after you with that doesn't he?" she bellowed and John tried to smile but couldn't.

"Not that again, woman. I thought that was last week's gripe."

Alone in his cupboard, Will finished scratching down his thoughts. He removed the wool pads from his ears, stretched, gathered up his manuscript and taking his cloak from the peg he left his room. On his way out he passed his father and spoke for the first time that day.

"I've finished it Dad. Fancy a pint to celebrate?"

"That's just what I could do with." This time his father smiled.

This was the last straw for her. The sparks began to fly again. "So you're off now are you. Leaving me alone after all I've done for you both. What's it called this time?"

"The Taming of the Shrew."

"What rubbish. You couldn't even catch one of the little blighters. I always knew you were an idiot. Mark my words. It'll never sell."

by Mary Pooley

The Chimbley Boy Done Good

Everyone in the borough was aware that Joe Whackerby, the chimney sweep, was heavy handed with his boys. Indeed, were it not for the soot covering their undernourished bodies, one would be able to see the bruises where they had made contact. And so, because it was rarely seen, few knew that beneath Joe Whackerby's harsh outward demeanour, there lurked a cushion of unexpected feathery kindness.

It was therefore remarked upon when Tommy Fairlad left the old bakery with a song in his throat and a hop skip and a jump in his bare feet as he made his way down Guttersnipe Lane towards the docks. The white of his eyes sparkled from his soot-blackened face and the rough cobblestones gave scant bother to the soles of his feet, which had never had the good fortune to feel soft leather. He kicked aside rotting vegetables tossed from a wooden barrow and hopped over putrid fish heads thrown from the filleting slabs of the fishmonger, their bulging eyes staring up sightless towards the blue sky. He was hard-pressed to keep his balance when he reached the slaughterhouse, where animal blood drained from a trench, giving a blush to the cobbles and splashing Tommy's legs, making a powdery mush as it mixed with layers of thick black soot from the bakery chimneys.

Once on the dockside, Tommy went from one ship to another until he found a vessel deserted by the crew, who were no doubt carousing in the Fourwinds Tavern and getting gloriously drunk. He scrambled up the gangplank and onto the deck, where he proceeded to remove his clothes. When he stood as naked as the day he was born, though much more grubby, he threw all his clothes overboard and dived in after them. Treading water, he rubbed and scrubbed at them until they were passably clean, before swimming round the dock until he too was passably clean, and pink. Climbing back on board, his clothes were soon laid out beside him on the deck, drying nicely in the sun as he pondered his good fortune.

"You done good," old Joe Whackerby had told him after he had boxed his ears a couple of times to show he hadn't lost the knack. "You really done good today, boy." He thrust a podgy fore-finger and thumb into a waistcoat pocket. "Yus, you done good. Now 'ere ye 'are, take this and keep your trap shut, unnerstand?"

"Yus Mister Whackerby, I unnerstand," and gripping seven coins tight in his mitt, he had scampered off before the master could change his mind. He was rich! He had never before had more than two coins in his whole life.

Lying on the deck in the sunshine was pleasing after the cramped confines of the bakery chimney, and he slept until the sailors returned and turfed him off their ship. "If you wuz bigger we'd shanghai ya, ya cheeky little whipper snapper," they said. Grabbing up his clothes he ran, quickly dressing on the dockside. He went into the Fourwinds Tavern and bought a jug of gin, then on to Molly Foyle's sweetshop. His mouth watered as he gazed at row upon row of gob stoppers, black and white striped mint balls, barley sugar, sherbet dabs, jelly babies and others too numerous to list. He had never ventured into a more serious transaction than the purchase of a halfpennyworth of dolly mixtures, or a few pieces of pan cooked toffee, which Molly cracked from the pan with a little silver hammer. Today, however, he handed over three pence and she put three newspaper cones of sweets on the wooden counter

"You didn't steal that money from your ma?" she asked with a wide Irish grin.

"Nah. Mister Whackerby said I done good, an' gived me extra," he told her. He walked on up the cobbled street until he came to the laundry. You could always tell when you were getting close because steam poured out of the huge boilers. He sat on the wall opposite the entrance and waited until the whistle blew and his mother came out of the big metal laundry gates, her face red and shiny from the atmosphere inside.

"What you got there, Tom?" she asked brushing sweat from her brow with her sleeve.

"I bought you a jug of gin, Ma."

"Crikey son, where'd ya get the money?"

"Mr Whackerby said I done good and gived me extra."

"You'd best do good every day then," she said, patting his head as if he were a dog. She took a slurp from the jug of gin and beamed at the lad.

That night they had meat and potatoes for supper instead of the usual bread and soup.

"So what you done so good for Mr Whackerby that he gived you extra then?" his ma asked.

"The bakery be closed for a week to clean all the chimblies," Tom said, his tongue scooping the last drop of gravy from his tin plate. "An when I was half way up the longest and the tallest chimbley I found Arthur Crumble stuck fast in one of the ledges. He been there since day before yesterday."

"Yeah, I can believe that, he's as plump as a pudden. Didn't his ma miss him then?

"Nah, she thought he'd runned away again."

"And was he all right?"

"He staggered about for a bit like he was drunk. Mr Whackerby sat him down on a bench, washed his face and gave him some milk an' a piece of bread and told him he was sending him to his bruvver's farm to clear the soot from his lungs. He'd find him another job as he was too fat now to be a chimbley boy.

Tom's mother pondered. Suppose the bakery fires had been re-lit before Tommy had discovered Arthur Crumble wedged in the chimney? She shivered, finished her jug of gin, and thought how very fortunate it was that her Tommy had done good that day.

by Barbara O Smith

Shakespeare Wordsearch

C	H	O	R	A	T	I	O	B	A	L	Y	I	N	S
E	T	A	P	U	C	K	Q	O	G	D	O	T	O	C
M	A	R	M	B	A	L	U	T	A	E	R	A	C	E
A	J	D	O	L	M	A	E	T	C	L	I	T	R	L
C	R	E	T	I	E	R	X	O	A	R	C	H	E	T
B	A	N	H	P	L	T	D	M	P	W	K	I	S	Y
E	O	B	E	W	C	U	E	Q	U	A	F	F	S	O
T	J	U	L	I	E	T	S	I	L	N	T	A	I	N
H	T	A	L	Y	S	O	D	S	E	T	I	R	D	E
K	I	G	O	C	H	V	E	H	T	O	T	B	A	P
O	T	E	F	R	I	X	M	O	U	N	A	R	S	U
M	A	A	L	O	N	S	O	S	H	Y	L	O	C	K
O	N	P	S	M	E	U	N	I	A	M	E	J	G	O
W	I	C	K	E	R	B	A	D	P	O	R	T	I	A
D	A	Z	H	O	F	A	L	S	T	A	F	F	E	D

The names of twenty Shakespearean characters are hidden in this Wordsearch. Can you find them?

They are listed on page 91.

12

A Midsummer's Nightmare

"Keeping you up are we, Whittaker?" came the sarcastic tones of the English teacher across a soporifically humid A-level classroom one afternoon towards the end of June. Tom Whittaker's drooping eyelids forced themselves open and he saw the face of Mr. Edmunds a few inches from his own.

"So sorry to interrupt your reverie, Whittaker," continued the master, "but if it's all the same to you I'd like your opinion on whether King Lear was more sinned against than sinning."

'Oh, God,' thought Tom. 'If only he knew'. But he must never know.

Four months before, Tom's mother, Rita, had walked out of the family home, fed up with her husband's philandering, leaving seventeen-year old Tom and his father, Reg, to fend for themselves. It had not been easy, and Tom's mountain of school work had been augmented by household chores which, he now realised, had to be done by someone and did not do themselves. Reg was a lorry driver, working shifts and irregular hours and, more often than not, if Tom wanted something to eat he had to prepare it himself. Reg usually ate in a cafe somewhere en route. Shopping, cleaning, cooking, laundry, history, English, and geography prep made a formidable list which left Tom permanently tired.

Then she had moved in. About three weeks after Rita's departure Reg walked in with a tarty-looking woman on his arm.

"This is Lily," announced Reg baldly to Tom, "she's moving in." In one glance Tom took in her long peroxide blonde hair, falling just below her shoulders, her large bust and backside, tattooed legs and heavily made-up face, and disliked her instantly. He reckoned she was about thirty-five, but looked twenty years older.

"Hi," grunted Tom, not moving from where he stood at the kitchen table.

"Right, babe," said Reg to Lily with a knowing look, "let me show you upstairs." Tom watched in both shock and horror as the couple hurried up the stairs, the bedroom door closed with a bang, and then followed noises which left little to the imagination. Tom flamed with anger. How dare his father bring a trollop like that home? How dare he?

Tom was cool towards Lily and kept out of her way as much as possible. She contributed little to the household both in terms of effort and money, slumming round the house all day, often with a bottle of gin or whisky, and invariably a cigarette.

"I can't work because of my back, love," she explained to Tom. 'Probably on it too much,' Tom thought, but did not voice his thoughts.

Then, after a fortnight, it started. Tom was in the shower before walking the mile or so to his High School in Ashington, and had not locked the bathroom door which suddenly opened. In the doorway stood Lily, her flimsy negligee hanging open at the front, revealing her ample breasts. "Wow, who's a big boy then," she smirked.

"What d'you think you're doing?" shouted Tom. "Get out of here."

"Now now," said Lily smoothly, walking over to the shower and appraising Tom's naked body approvingly. He was a good-looking young lad, with a mop of tousled brown hair, powerful physique and a fine six pack. She ran her hand over his chest, causing a sudden stirring within him and an involuntary movement lower down.

"Not now, young Tom," she murmured, "your dad will be home soon. There'll be another time. Oh yes, there'll be another time".

That time came all too soon as, two mornings later when Reg was away overnight on a long haul, Lily suddenly appeared in Tom's bedroom doorway and made her way across to his bed where he lay naked and drowsy.

"OK, Tom," Lily purred, "time to make you a man," dropping her housecoat and standing unclothed before him. She looked gross, thought Tom, as he started awake and sat up, shifting away from her. But Lily sat on his bed and then lay across him, running her hands across his body. He could smell the drink on her breath from the night before and wanted to get away, yet the touch of Lily's hands roused him in a way he had never experienced as strongly before and, unable to resist, in a hot and clumsy tangle he gave way. It was over almost as quickly as it started, but Lily seemed satisfied. "Not bad for a first time, Tom," she grinned. "It'll be better next time!"

Next time? Next time? Tom was furious at his seduction, although he had to admit some satisfaction after the act, but he had really wanted Claire, his girlfriend of six months, a pretty, auburn haired young lass whose passion was growing, like his. He knew it would not be long before they 'did it'. Lily heaved herself off his bed. "This is our little secret, Tom, " she said. "We don't want your father finding out, do we? I'd have to tell him you forced yourself upon me, and we wouldn't want that, would we?" Tom knew only too well from experience what his father was like when angry. Many were the clouts round the head and, sometimes, the feel of the belt when Reg was annoyed and drunk. But there was not going to be a next time; of that he was certain.

Tom missed his mother. As Lear said of his daughter, Cordelia, 'her voice was soft and low, an excellent thing in woman', unlike the coarse mouthed slag who was now his father's partner, more like one of the witches in Macbeth. Tom despised her, as he despised himself for yielding to her advances. He had demeaned himself and let his mother down, but Lily's advances had proved too strong for him to overcome.

The following day was Sunday and Tom's father announced that they would spend the day at Alnwick Castle as Lily had never been there.

"You can drive, Tom," he said. " It's only twenty-odd miles and it will be good practice before your test next month. I had a fair bit to drink last night and can't risk being picked up by the police. I'd lose my job."

Walking round the grounds they came across the Poison Garden. "Ooh, a poison garden!" shouted Lily. "Can we have a look round there? I might find something to do you in with, Reg," she giggled, and they both laughed. Tom did not laugh, but looked thoughtful. The guide was insistent that they touched nothing in the garden, explaining how deadly the plants were if not used properly.

"This one is atropa belladonna, sleeping nightshade, which Friar Laurence used to drug Juliet and make her appear dead. It can actually stop the heart sometimes, and it grows in our hedgerows. This one is aconitum, monk's hood, which can be poisonous if it comes into contact with cuts and open wounds. Neither leaves any trace."

"Blimey!" exclaimed Lily. "I never knew there was as many nasty plants in the world."

Lily and Reg passed through the exit gate. "Come on, Tom," called Reg, as Tom was hanging behind, "there's plenty more to see."

They looked at the gardens, cascade and fountains, but as they walked through one of the wilder areas Lily tripped, stepped into some nettles, and scratched her leg on some brambles. "Ow!" she cried, rubbing her leg in pain. "Them nettles don't half sting."

"Here," called Tom, let's put some dock leaves on it, they always ease stings," and he foraged in the long grass and wrapped some leaves across the sting and the wound and tied it with a handkerchief. Later, back at the car Tom removed the makeshift bandage as the blood had stopped, and threw away the wilted leaves.

After another few days of Lily doing little but drink and lounge around the house, Tom and Reg arrived home simultaneously on the Friday evening. The television was on with Lily sitting in front of it. Something about her made them both stop as they entered the room. Lily's mouth was agape and her eyes stared sightlessly at the television. A bottle of whisky lay spilt in her lap with a broken glass beside the chair. Tom and Reg looked at each other.

"She got drunk and boasted what she'd done to you, the bitch," said Reg. "It's one thing with me, but to do that to my son...." his voice trailed off. "So I - "

"Dad, don't," interrupted Tom. "It must have been when -"

"That's enough, Tom." This time Reg stopped his son.

The sudden, unexplained death meant police involvement, but after the autopsy and all the investigations the coroner recorded a verdict of accidental death, with alcohol a contributory factor.

Tom snapped out of his reverie and his eyes focused on Mr. Edmunds' unpleasant countenance. "Sorry, sir. In my opinion, given what those women did to him, King Lear was certainly more sinned *against* than sinning."

by David Baldock

Crumpled fallen leaf
transformed to jewelled beauty
by streetlight and frost.

I watch the red kite
skating across the wintry sky
suddenly it's spring.

16

Man Cave

"Stupid Cow!"

Josh slammed the door of his shed, stepped over a carpet of discarded cans and slumped into his deckchair. His fingers searched for a full can from the pile beside his chair.

"Watch it mate!"

Josh snatched his hand away and peered down at his neatly arranged pyramid of lager. He shook his head, he was hearing things but not one drop of amber liquid had passed his lips...yet. "Who said that?" He felt stupid addressing an empty space.

"I did. Look down here."

He directed his gaze to the floor and gasped. "What the... who are you?"

The tiny figure, legs straddled and arms akimbo, fixed Josh with a steely glare. "I am Oberon, King of the Fairies."

"And I'm Prince Charles," Josh retorted.

"You are not your ears are too small."

Leaving his chair Josh got down on his knees.

"There's no need to kneel before me – I'm incognito at the moment."

"I'm not bloody kneeling to you I'm trying to get a better look at you."

Josh surveyed the perfectly formed man fairy dressed, not in gossamer and golden threads but a pair of ragged jeans and a leather jacket.

"Where are your wings?"

The fairy sighed, shrugged off his jacket and flexed his biceps. Immediately a pair of majestic wings sprouted from his back.

"Now you believe I'm a fairy because I've got wings?"

Josh nodded and returned to his chair. The fairy flew on to the bench opposite, folded his wings and pulled his jacket on. "You have trouble with a cow?" he asked.

"What? Oh no, I was referring to my wife."

"I've got one of those."

"A cow or a wife?"

"A wife, Titania."

"If I remember my Shakespeare isn't she Queen of the Fairies?"

"She is, and doesn't she know it, her and her silly little followers, flitting around the palace, giggling all the time."

Josh opened a can of lager. "Sorry I've nothing to offer you."

"Don't worry about it I've my own tipple." Oberon pulled out a tiny

17

hip flask from his jeans and took a swig. "That's better." He wiped his mouth with the back of his hand. "Nectar," he grinned.

"So these giggling fairies?"

"Don't get me started – Mustard Seed, Eglantine, such stupid names. They all fly off to a bank in the woods where the wild thyme blows. Puck knows what they get up to there."

Josh laughed. "My wife, Tiffany belongs to some book club. Sounds more like a Witches coven if you ask me."

Oberon backed away. "Witches, where be these witches?"

Josh laughed. "Not real witches, although I sometimes think my mother-in-law is a witch."

"My mother-in-law is a witch."

"Sorry, I didn't mean to offend."

"I'm not offended – she's a crabby old woman who only comes to visit once a year on Midsummer's night and I keep out of her way."

"I know the feeling, that's what our argument was about, Tiff wants her mother to come and stay for a week."

"Commiserations, but this book club your wife attends, what is a book club?"

"A group of her pals, bit like your wife's fairy friends I should think, meet two nights a week to discuss a book they've been reading. More like an excuse for wine and gossip if you ask me. Anyway, I think they're reading Fifty Shades of Grey at the moment and I can tell you it gives them ideas. I find it best not to take the lift with her in John Lewis at present."

Oberon shrugged. "Tanya, that's what I call her in private, had this thing about a man with the head of a donkey. Took him to her bower – that's where I caught her stroking his fur so I told him in no uncertain terms to hoof off. Now we're not talking and that's why I'm hiding in your shed."

"You're welcome." Josh opened another can. "So this King lark, is it any good?"

Oberon jumped from the bench and perched on an empty lager can. "Most of the time I enjoy it. But what about you? I've noticed you spend a lot of your time in here."

"Have you been spying on me?"

Oberon laughed. "Not spying, just remaining invisible. See." Josh blinked, there was no sign of Oberon. "And back in the room," the fairy laughed.

"That's a neat trick I could do with some of that magic."

"Sorry, not available to humans." He gestured to the pyramid of cans. "You get through a lot of those in a day."

"Well she's enough to drive me to drink." Josh rubbed his nose. "But for all that I wouldn't change her."

"I feel the same about Tanya, she flits around putting on airs and graces but I love her."

"To be fair, she is entitled to airs and graces, she is a queen."

"True, but I'm King and therefore she should obey me."

"I'm guessing that doesn't happen often."

Oberon folded his arms, shaking his head. "Sadly, no."

"You should be more assertive, stand up for yourself, tell her who's boss."

The fairy leapt to his feet. "You're right. After all I have the right to demand obedience."

"Word to the wise old man, be less bullish about it, treat her gently but firmly."

"So, that's how you treat your Tiffany?"

Josh spluttered into his can of drink. "Well..."

"Come on, if I can show Tanya who's boss surely you can tell your wife who wears the trousers?"

"Problem is she wears trousers most of the time."

"Well you know what I mean."

"Yes, we can both do it, let the women know who rules the roost."

Josh discovered trying to high five a fairy was difficult but they managed after a fashion.

"Time I was off, I promised to take Tiff shopping this afternoon."

Oberon unfolded his wings and gave Josh a wink. "Don't go taking the lift."

Josh grinned. "We'll take the stairs."

He walked to the door. "It was great meeting you Oberon, good luck with the missus and feel free to visit my man cave any time. I thoroughly enjoyed our chat."

"Likewise, and thank you for your hospitality."

Josh carefully closed the shed door and walked slowly towards the house. Had he been chatting to a fairy? He grinned, he really had. He decided to dig out his old school copy of "A Midsummer's Night Dream" just so that he had more to talk about when he next met up with Oberon.

One thing he was certain about, he would not mention Oberon to Tiff. She would never believe they had fairies at the bottom of their garden.

by Joyce Robinson

Glad Tidings We Bring

The mantel clock ticked loudly in the gloomy parlour as a voice boomed out, 'Squidgebucket, Squidgebucket, where are you?'

A scrawny man looking not unlike a ruffled quill pen shuffled in, 'I'm here Mr Dickens.'

'Squidgebucket, have you seen my Dictionary of Silly Names?'

Squidgebucket scratched at his unkempt head of straggly hair and then at his whiskery beard, and then shook his head and studied the dandruff snow-shower as it sprinkled to the floor. 'No Mr Dickens.'

Charles Dickens gazed at the falling snow, 'Squidgebucket, what is the point of me having a clerk if you don't know where my dictionary is? Where do you think my characters silly names come from, do you think I just make them up?'

'Actually sir that's what I thought writers d . . .' he stopped himself in mid sentence, 'I'll look for it now sir, and to aid my search may I turn on more gas lamps?'

'MORE, did you say MORE, Squidgebucket?'

'Yes, more lamps if you please sir.'

'MORE. You ungrateful wretch.'

'No offence sir, but it is very gloomy and this is such a bleak house.'

Dickens stood with his thumbs wedged in his waistcoat pockets, scraping his shoe across the snow-like heap on the floor. 'Bleak House, mmh, Bleak House, now there's a thought. Right off you go Squidgebucket, and find that dictionary; I'm running out of silly names.'

Dickens then rushed to his study and scribbled on his pad, "Bleak House, and remember not to sack Squidgebucket". He then sat at his desk and stared at the wall as he did most days, waiting for inspiration.

Ten minutes later Squidgebucket knocked on his study door.

'Come in.'

Begging your pardon Mr Dickens, I have found your dictionary, and there is a gentleman to see you.'

'And pray Squidgebucket, does this gentleman have a name?'

'I may have misheard sir but I think it's Heap sir, Urinal Heap.'

'Urinal Heap eh Squidgebucket, are you taking the . . . . Oh never mind, show him in.'

A pasty Mr Heap came to the study and stood porcelain-faced at the door.

Dickens stood to shake hands but on second thoughts decided against.

'How may I help you Mr Heap, or should I call you Urinal.'

'As you wish your eminence. Well sir you can help me in so many ways, but I crave of just one favour on behalf of the townsfolk.' Heap then dropped to his knees in a most subservient manner.

Dickens was about to ask him to stand when he decided he rather liked his new found eminence and instead asked, 'What is it the townsfolk want of me?'

'They have requested sir that you stop poking the workhouse boys up their chimneys?'

'This is no time for euphemisms Heap.'

'I meant no euphemism sir. The townsfolk are most concerned. And when the poor mites get stuck and you light a fire to encourage them upwards their howling through the night is most disturbing.'

'But that is the whole point Urinal, I need to capture the atmosphere of those terrible moments. I am a writer, how else am I to write with realism, just make it up?'

Heap looked up at Dickens, 'Actually sir that's what I thought writers d . .' He stopped in mid sentence. 'Of course not sir, I completely see your point, how foolish of me.' His knees were now aching and he asked, 'May I stand now sir.'

'If you must,' Dickens said.

Heap creaked himself upright, 'Perhaps I can ask if the wee mites may have a break for this coming Christmas holiday sir.'

'But that's my busiest time, Heap, and I have Tiny Tim lined up for a very narrow chimney in Deptford tomorrow.'

'Oh no sir, not Tiny Tim sir, not up a chimney sir, I beg you.' He dropped to his knees again, his hands locked as if in prayer. Then an idea came to him, as if his prayer had been answered. 'Might I suggest instead sir that you send up Little Dorrit. She's not known as Little for no reason and she'd be up there like a rat up a drainpipe, if you'll forgive the cliché, sir.'

'Cliché forgiven, Heap, and that's not such a poor idea. I'll think on it.'

Squidgebucket then returned to the room, 'Begging your pardon sir but it's getting late and you want me to purchase your Christmas gifts today.'

Dickens clapped his hand to his forehead, 'Spend, spend, spend. I hate this time of the year Squidgebucket. I should be in my parlour counting my money, not sending you out to spend it for me.'

Heap creaked himself upright again, 'I'll be leaving you now sir, and thank you most kindly for allowing me to kneel before you.'

'Off you go Heap. And don't forget to work hard this Christmas, this is no time for holidays, is it Squidgebucket?'

Squidgebucket, who had hoped for an hour off on Christmas Day, mumbled, 'Of course not Mr Dickens.'

Dickens waited until Heap had left the room and then asked Squidgebucket, 'What gifts did I buy last year?

'Handkerchiefs sir, from your old friend Mr Fagin, he has such a wonderful range of colours and sizes.'

'Ah yes Fagin. But he's getting a bit pricey. Before you go to Mr Fagin check out the prices in that new store opposite Ye Olde Curiosity Shoppe.'

'I know the one sir, Ye Olde Primarkey.'

'That's the one, Squidgebucket. And choose a handkerchief for yourself, nothing too large mind.'

'Oh thank you Mr Dickens, but I had no great expectations.'

'No what Squidgebucket?'

'Great expectations, sir.'

'Quite so. Now be off with you, I've just had an idea and must write it down.'

by Les Williams

A
coke tin
thrown away
between the takes,
rolls towards shelter from the desert sun.
An
extra
waves his hat
to cool his face.
The filming goes on somewhere in the shade.

The Scottish Play

Sometimes I wonder about my sanity. Why do I always agree to do things when I should gently refuse? When Mark, the young fellow who happens to sit in the desk next to mine at work asked me to take part in the play he was producing I naively said "perhaps." He then proceeded to nag me for the next fortnight until eventually I used the word "yes." I, perhaps rather stupidly, did not ask what the play would be, I did not ask what part he visualised me playing, and in fact I mumbled my agreement merely to shut him up. I was being conscientious about this large contract my boss was hoping to win and my mind was on other things. The fact was that Mark knew I'd been in quite a number of semi-professional productions way back in the nineties and he rather presumed I was good at acting. How little did he know?

Anyway at his request the following Friday I went to the audition and discovered the play was Shakespeare's Scottish Play (in the Theatre it is bad luck to actually use the title name). The Little Futtock Players met in the village hall and when I arrived twenty men and women sat around and looked expectantly at me. Mark had obviously spread the news of my acting ability. There was some discussion before we began the reading and at Mark's request I read the main part. Believe me I did not read well but sadly the other ten hopeful men who read later were even worse hams than me. Later as we all gathered around Mark stood up clearly very satisfied "I think we all agree there can only be one person good enough to be play our hero." A murmur of approval went around the room and we all went across to the George and Dragon pub to celebrate my triumph. I went shaking my head in disbelief. My mind was in rather a whirl and my fellow actors generously showed their lack of jealousy by buying me a great number of drinks. In a way they helped me drown my anxieties.

I am ashamed to admit that I had to be helped back to my flat. Staggering to my bedroom I took off my clothes and sank into my bed. Sleep came easily. Then the unbelievable happened because the Ghost of Shakespeare came to me. I know it sounds ridiculous but it happened. Naturally I sobered up immediately. Who wouldn't when Shakespeare's Ghost visits them?

"Hiya," he said "I believe you have been selected to play Macbeth in my play. I hear you weren't much cop, too."

"No I wasn't very good."

"My source reckoned you were bleeding awful."

I was still stretched out on my bed but I decided I had better get up and take a better look at my unexpected guest. So I sat on my bed and stared at him. He was dressed with a doublet kind of thing and terrible baggy tights that were full of holes. Possibly unsurprisingly he was covered in cobwebs.

"You look terrible," I couldn't help exclaiming.

"I haven't been out for years," he whinged.

"Why not?"

"It's a kind of rote thing where we only come down to see you guys when things are desperate."

"I didn't realise they were?"

"I guess not but you do need help."

This was obviously true because although I didn't want to be in the play I definitely didn't want to let down Mark or the rest of the Little Futtock Players. Tentatively I asked Shakespeare what he thought I should do.

"Way back when my Players asked me a question like that I would always say, "You have got to surprise your audience. Have a bloke hiding behind a curtain stabbed or let your heroine go mad. That kind of thing."

"But everyone knows Mac…. the Scottish Play. How can you have surprises in it?"

"That is a problem but I do have some kind of solution. A notion whereby you can be a little bit different."

"That sounds interesting?"

"Yes I was talking to my good friend Liberace the other day. Do you recall Liberace."?

"The piano player but he died some years ago."

"Don't be stupid, of course he did that is why I was talking to him."

"Sorry."

"Anyway I was chatting to Liberace and he came up with a bright idea. "What if," he said "Macbeth were gay". It was like a revelation to me. Macbeth as a gay man…brilliant."

Naturally this idea came as a shock to me. All sorts of objections came into my brain.

"But what about Lady Macbeth? They were married?"

"Ah it has happened over the years. Oscar Wilde was married before the events in his life took an ugly turn. I have spoken to him about it and he merely regrets living in the time that he did. But getting back to Macbeth I have no doubt it was an arranged marriage. He married her for her lands or something like that. Listen, my time is nearly up so I am away now. Think about it."

"Just one question how come you speak in a twenty-first century manner?"

"One has to move with the times one has to be or not to be."

With that Shakespeare went and the next thing I knew the sun was shining through my bedroom window. It was morning.

For the next few days I mulled over this idea from Shakespeare. As I have already mentioned I had done a little acting, although I was mostly an assistant stage manager, and I knew you have to find the character of the part you are going to play. Sometimes it is a small thing like the hat your character wears. I remember reading that Alec Guinness needed to stumble on some quirk before he could feel at home playing a part.

We were due to meet the following Friday and I well remember the look on the faces of the Little Futtock Players when I revealed that my Macbeth was to be gay. My Lady Macbeth, a young well-built lady, possibly fifteen stone in weight, did go rather pale. However, when I explained how novel our version of the play was to be then the faces of my fellow cast members did brighten a little.

Over the next three months we had weekly rehearsals and I must say how I really got into the part playing Macbeth as a more effeminate version of Julian Clary. My Lady Macbeth rose to the occasion too with a character not unlike Miranda Hart. When the opening night arrived we were absolutely amazed at the size of the audience. The village hall was packed. I suspect the Fire Officer at our local Fire Station would have been horrified if he had happened to stroll in and found people sitting in the aisles.

The opening scenes passed quickly especially as we had cut a few lines because we only had one witch. Then it was my turn.

"Macbeth doth come." The witch cried out.

I came on wearing a pink tunic and matching tights. "Thow foul and fair a day I have not theen." I cried. There was complete silence. The audience were clearly stunned. We staggered on through the play with absolutely no audience reaction whatsoever apart from the odd snigger or two. Eventually I cried out to McDuff "Hold enough" and some one shouted out "So say all of us."

There was not a lot of chatter in the dressing room as we removed our make-up. I thought I really should say something "it went quite well didn't it…I mean no one forgot their lines," I muttered. Silence.

We did three more performances but sadly the audiences dwindled.

On the Monday following I went into the office as usual and was rather taken aback when Mark came rushing up to me. "Guess what?" he shouted. I had no idea what he going to drop me in next.

"Larry Bullough Quinn has been in touch," he yelled.

"Who is he?

"Have you never heard of him? He is that famous West End producer who puts on all that experimental avant-garde stuff."

"Well?"

"He wants to put our Macbeth on at his Empirical Theatre and he wants you to star in it."

As Shakespeare might have said it was "such stuff as nightmares are made of."

by Les Cooper

Mea culpa

By Colin Ferguson

One final touch, then "Stand clear of the doors",
face at the window and a gentle wave
sent each of us upon a different course,
left her with words I never quite forgave,
in tears that had no time left to complain.
I saw them as I sent her on her way,
upon her own as love discovered pain.
Too late I thought of what I ought to say
and stood there shamed by her soft parting tears,
hid in the steam and bit my errant tongue.
My clumsiness has echoed through the years
and never found excuse for being young.
She did not write, no questions, no complaint;
I took her silence as my own constraint.

Uncle

I didn't believe mum when she said that nursing wouldn't suit me. Even so I thought I'd give it a go as I'd quite liked caring for my bed-ridden Nan. There weren't that many other lads on the course and it wasn't that tough. I managed to get a junior job at the local nursing home in Dover and was put on the Albany ward. Cathy, a nurse who joined on the same day, called it the 'Dim ward' as they were all dementia patients; half the time they looked more dead than alive with their glazed eyes and gaping mouths. The other nurses seemed to only shout orders at them. When I spent time trying to understand what it was they wanted, I was told to get a move on. So I was beginning to get a bit pissed off with nursing. One day that all changed, I was making up Mr. Vaughan's bed with Cathy, fooling around as usual, doing my impersonation of the manager which always made her laugh. Mr. Vaughan was sitting in his chair and I could see him smiling. He was a fairly slim and wiry old man with scattered grey hair surrounding his bald head. He spoke to me for the first time when later I brought him a mug of tea.

'Young man, can I ask your name?'

'Sure, my name's Tom, Tom Edmondson.'

'I wonder, Tom, could I ask you a favour? If you ever have any free time can you come and read to me?' he asked with a plaintive look.

'No problem' I replied. I kept my word and my readings with him became a regular fixture. I enjoyed bringing the books to life; it made him laugh which encouraged me to over-act outrageously. One day he told me how much he was appreciating it.

'Thanks Mr. Vaughan.' I said.

'Tom you are such an honest hearted fellow; please just call me Leonard.'

'That's not right; you're as old as my granddad. How about if I call you "Uncle"?'

'That'll do fine.'

From then on I started spending more time with 'uncle'. I noticed that whenever women came into his room he clammed up and the life seemed to drain out of him. He had only one visitor who came once every couple of months, a posh looking old man who always looked rather upset. All uncle would say about him was that he came from Gloucester and that he had no relatives. So I thought I ought to find out more about him, surely there must be someone else to come and visit him?

It wasn't hard to take a peep at his records. I tricked the manager's secretary out of the office for a moment and took pictures on my iPhone. Later when I looked them over I was shocked to read that there were three daughters listed as next of kin. The notes said that two of them had originally brought him to the home. The next week the ward sister asked me into her office; I wondered if she had found out about my detective work.

'As you continue to spend too much time with Leonard Vaughan, I had planned to transfer you to another ward, but that won't now be necessary as Leonard will be leaving us.'

'Leaving the nursing home?'

'Yes, it seems two of his daughters have found somewhere else; apparently considerably cheaper. It's the Aldridge Nursing Home at Folkestone.'

'But it's miles from Dover; an awful place. He can't go there.'

'That is not up to us Tom, his daughters have decided.'

I couldn't bear to lose my only friend on the ward. My only idea was to contact his third daughter, Claudia, to see if she could persuade the others to change their minds. I had misgivings about phoning her, but as mum says 'nothing will come from nothing', so I rang Claudia and persuaded her to meet up. I suggested Greggs in Station Road and she was sitting there waiting for me. She had fair hair in loose curls and was wearing quite posh clothes.

'Hello Tom, please take a seat. What is all this about father?'

'Your sisters want to move him, but I know he'll hate it. It's not right, he's still totally 'with it' if you know what I mean.'

'No I don't.'

'Well the others can't hold a sensible conversation, not for long anyway. Some can barely speak, but your dad's still all there.'

'I had no idea. I had thought he had advanced dementia, that's what my sisters said.'

'You'd know straight away if you saw him.'

'But he doesn't want to see me, he made that abundantly clear. You must think me horrid, not visiting but believe me I have tried. I applied to the Court of Protection to get the address, but my sisters blocked me at every turn. I fought them as hard as I could but as they are the court's appointed deputies they can do whatever they like. They say father wants no contact with me and the court took their side.'

'They sound totally vile, how did it happen?'

'When he retired as chief executive of the family firm they made a great scene about how much they cared. However that was only until they persuaded him to sign over all his rights and assets to them. Then they turned him out of the family house, had him sectioned, and here he is.'

'That's most savage and unnatural, couldn't you have stopped them?'

'No, he turned against all of us, even me, who cared about him the most.'

'I am sure you can persuade them, you must give it a try.'

We agreed to go to see him the following day, even though it was breaking all the rules.

'Uncle, I have brought in someone to see you.' I said with Claudia following me into the room.

Mr. Vaughan was sitting in his tattered dressing gown on his bed. He made a smile that soon disappeared when he caught sight of Claudia.

'Father.'

'I have no children.'

'Father, I know I let you down, but that is all over now.' said Claudia sitting down next to him on the bed. 'Rebecca and Geraldine want to move you to some awful place, I intend to stop them.'

'It makes no difference. A man may rot even here.'

'Father, I said I loved you no more than was your right, is that my crime? You must know that you have total right over me, you always had my full affection.' Uncle's eyes began to shine as they gazed directly at her.

'Is my viper's brood clean out of venom?'

'That is not quite fair. I think you expected too much from us, how could we ever have matched the dreams you had set for us? My so-called sisters put you here to conceal their shame in falling short. We should have spoken plainly. Now we shall speak what we feel, not what we ought to say.'

'And you are different from them? I, your old, kind father whose frank heart gave all.'

'But I sought your love - not your wealth and power.'

'How sharper than a serpent's tooth it is to have a thankless child!'

'Come father, I mean to take you away. While I still can. Come, give me your hand.'

'While you still can, what do you mean?' he asked staring hard at Claudia, giving her his arm, she grasped it warmly, tears running down her pretty cheeks.

'Father, we must make the most of this short time. For I...' she broke off to gather her composure. 'Have come far too late. They gave me a few short weeks, that is all, the chemotherapy did not work.' She hung her head amid her copious tears.

'My child, to gain and then to lose you. No! It is too much, too much!'

At this Mr. Vaughan gave out a loud wail and started sobbing uncontrollably.

'Father, stop your tears.'

'But I have full cause for weeping.'

With a second despairing shriek his body swayed and fell into Claudia's arms.

I knew it was the end; they said it was from heart failure. Not long after Mr. Vaughan's funeral, Claudia died just as she had predicted. I lost my job because of what had happened and I gave up nursing; mum had been proven right after all. When I was thinking about what I should do next I remembered uncle suggesting I should give drama school a try, and so that is what I am doing and I love every minute.

by Rob Stallard

Sudoku

Complete the grid so that every row, column and 3x3 box contains the letters EGIKLNOTU in any order.

One row or column contains the seven-letter name of a writer.

Who is it?

		E				U		
	L			K	I			
K		I		O				
		O	G				E	
I			O		N			L
	T				K	G		
				U		E		T
			L	G			O	
		L				N		

Answer on page 91.

Good Works in the Times of Charles Dickens

The smartly dressed, good looking, young man was ushered into the juror's room by the Beadle, making up the twelve jurors needed for the Coroners inquest. He could hear his fellow jurors, mainly local businessmen, discussing the case to be tried before they had had heard any evidence. They were to pronounce on a young servant girl who was said to have murdered her new born child. One juror was already loudly calling for 'the full rigor of the law to be applied to the perpetrator of this despicable act'.

As if to harden their hearts even further, the jurors were taken to the workhouse mortuary to see the dead infant before returning to the Coroner's court. The young woman, Eliza Burgess, was brought into the room by a workhouse nurse who she tried to hide behind. To the new young juror she looked weak, ill and frightened. He asked the coroner's permission to talk to her.

'Eliza,' he said in a quiet voice, how old are you?'

She stared at him with her timidness showing in her eyes.

'I don't know sir,' I was an orphan and nobody's told me when I was born. Twenty four or twenty five I think'.

'Tell us what happened to your baby Eliza'.

'I was in the kitchen of Mrs Symmons's house...'

'Mrs Symmons – that's your mistress is it?'

'Yes sir, well the bell rang and I hurried upstairs and let in two lady visitors. When I got back down to the kitchen I found the baby in my skirts, already born – and dead.'

'So what did you do next Eliza?'

She cast a hasty look around the court room. She seemed to be summoning the courage to tell the remainder of her story

'I had to cut the cord of course and then I cleaned up the best I could. I found a large box and I put my dead baby in and hid him under the dresser'.

'What happened then?'

'After Mrs Symmons's guests had left, she told me to scrub the front steps.'

'And did you do that?'

'No, she saw how ill I was and said to me 'you've given birth haven't you?'. I tried to pretend I hadn't but she said she would have me medically examined so I admitted it'.

'So you showed her your baby and what did she do then?'

'She sent me and the baby in a hansom cab to the workhouse infirmary.'

The first witness was Mrs Symmons who confirmed to the coroner that Eliza's story was basically true. Although the Coroner was happy for the young juror to speak to her, she refused to accept this, so he was unable to question her rather unsympathetic version of the events. However, the next witness, the house surgeon, Mr Boyd, after telling the coroner that there was no way to say positively whether the baby had been born dead or alive, agreed to be questioned by the young juror

'Is there a way that you normally know when a baby is born dead?'

'If there is foreign matter in its windpipe, it would suggest that it has taken at the most, a few breaths'.

'And did Eliza's baby have foreign matter in his windpipe?'

'I have to admit that it did,' replied the surgeon.

Eliza Burgess was then taken away while the jurors and the coroner discussed the case.

The young juror was determined to take on those who were ready to find her guilty and he did it with such force, aided by help from the coroner that the others finally agreed.

When the young woman was brought back to hear their verdict, she fell to her knees when she heard the coroner pronounce – 'found dead'.

'Thank you, thank you all, you are right, you are so right,' she cried, before she fainted and was carried away.

But that was not the end of the affair, for although she no longer faced the gallows, Eliza was still held under the charge of 'unlawfully concealing the birth of a male child'.

The young man's first act after parting from his fellow jurors was to send some food to the prison for the now relieved young woman. He had already seen many pitiful scenes in prisons. The next day he contacted an excellent barrister, Richard Doane, to defend her at her Old Bailey trial. This also led to the discovery of a crucial witness to her character. A Mr Clarkson, who said she had previously worked for his family and they were willing to take her back into their employ. He agreed to speak for her in court. This willingness of respectable people to help her was good for Eliza's cause and although the jury found her guilty of concealment, they strongly recommended mercy. The judge then let her free under certain conditions.

As she left the court she rushed up to Mr Doane and Mr Clarkson on the steps of the Old Bailey and thanked them profusely for enabling her release.

'This is the man you should be thanking', said Mr Doane, turning to the man standing next to him.

'Yes sir', she said facing him, 'I remember you treating me kindly in the coroner's court.'

'Not just that,' said Richard Doane, 'he sent you food in jail and he hired me to defend you in court today'.

'How can I ever replay you sir. First you saved my life and now you have given me hope for the future, And sir, I don't even know your name.'

'But Eliza,' said Mr Clarkson, 'this is the man who writes for the newspapers and magazines, Mr Dickens, Mr Charles Dickens.

by Dick Sawdon Smith

Light in Sway

Light swirls across a photograph,
vanilla rippling through blueberry ice.
Shivering I enter. I am surrounded,

not by paper but by silk.

A sandalwood fire burns unseen.
Smoke rising, drifts past me,
leaving only its fragrance.

I switch off the light.

All I see now is the camera,
pointing at me.
accusing me.

Shooting.

A Village in Kosovo

Kosovo late 1990's

Sultana sat in the deserted square listening to the distant sound of knelling bells that wafted across the bleak mountainside. They tolled in sympathy with the dual Muslim burial that was taking place nearby. A sunray darted across her face, and she remembered when those same bells rang in jubilation on a similar sunny day. They had rung for the marriage of one of their Christian Orthodox flock to Ali, an Albanian Muslim, in the village.

She wiped away a tear that spilled over onto her cheek. She walked over to the barrier that formed one side of the square and where the land fell precipitously to a plain below. How could such an ugly tragedy happen in this beautiful place? she wondered. She turned, on the left a rough road entered the square and exited on the opposite side. Beyond was a short surrounding band of flat land before the forest took over, but it failed to rise very high on the barren mountain that peaked against the sky.

She remembered the wedding, but only she and Murat knew the whole story which followed. The village had amassed in the square. Ali was so much in love – it showed in his eyes, in his smile, in his whole being. He was marrying Anna, an Orthodox Christian, from the next village. She'd converted to Islam and his happiness was only eclipsed by hers.

Murat and Ali had been inseparable since their boyhood and as they grew it matured into something closer than brotherhood. After the wedding, Ali disappeared for four days and Murat wandered around lost. Murat slouched in the coffee shop whiling away a few hours when Ali's muscular form reappeared crossing the square.

'Ali.'

Ali rushed over to Murat.

'Ali, have a coffee and we'll play some backgammon. I've missed you, old friend.'

'Murat, it warms my heart to see you. But no backgammon. I've got a wife to get home to. But come and eat with us whenever you want, my Anna's an angel-cook.'

Murat's thin face fell and his thin lips parted in disappointment. How alone Murat seemed. Then Ali thought of Anna, how they'd sit in the kitchen talking and laughing, his hand on hers, and the thought prodded him into a canter.

Sultana remembered these events with a shudder.

A few days later, Anna went into the baker's shop, in the square, and she rushed towards Murat's sister with her usual warm greeting. Murat's sister turned her back, picked up her bread, and walked out. Anna froze. The kindly baker's wife handed Anna her bread and took the money without a smile, muttering, 'Murat says there are non-Muslim subversives in our midst.' Anna felt the stab. Her heart seemed empty and her stomach raw. She walked along with her eyes downcast but then saw her dear friend Fata. Fata stared at her with icy eyes, then hurried off. As the days passed she was ostracized by all the women in the village. The feeling of isolation brought great sobs of breath from her. 'I don't want Ali to know. I want him to be proud of me as his accepted Muslim wife,' she whimpered. There was no one she could turn to except Sultana, her confidant, and to the refuge of the little Orthodox church, a short way down the mountain, there she could pray. Perhaps that would ease her hurt.

Sultana thought regretfully, I should have intervened then.

One afternoon Murat walked into Ali's metal workshop. 'Ali, Serb troops have marched into Kosovo. The Kosovo Liberation Army needs the support of every one of us now. If those Orthodox Serbs get to us it'll be murders and rape, imprisonment and they'll torch our houses. Remember Srebrenica and Zepa. They'll terrorize us to flee.'

Ali stood up to his full height, his face wrinkled into a frown. 'Where are the centuries of living in harmony gone?' he sighed.

'Gone forever. We must be sure there are no traitors in our midst. By the way, how's Anna?'

'Pregnant. I'm soon to have a son. How good that feels, Murat.' And he puffed out his chest.

'What does she do all day?'

'Cooking, cleaning,' Ali shrugged.

'Probably a mistake, but she was seen going to the Orthodox church today.'

'Impossible,' Ali replied.

When Ali reached home he opened the little door that led to the kitchen and his heart lurched. He took Anna in his arms and brushed some chestnut strands of hair off her face. I love you more than anything in this world Anna.' Her brown eyes smiled up at him feeling the security of his strong arms. 'What did you do today?'

'Cooking.'

'You didn't go out?'

Anna hesitated. Should she tell him about the women in the village?

35

Better not. 'No.' The lie made her stomach turn.

A son was born. Ali couldn't understand why the mid-wife didn't come. At last he went to her house and dragged her by her arm to the birth. He had never been happier. There were just two people in this world that he lived for. Could anything be more precious, more joyful?

Murat came with congratulations; he grabbed Ali in a bear hug saying, 'The hunting season begins on Saturday. I'll see you as always.'

'Not this year, Murat. I've got other duties.' Ali saw the disbelief in Murat's eyes as his jaw fell open.

'But we've never missed a season together.'

Ali shrugged.

Murat's face hardened. 'We think that the old Orthodox woman's hut in the woods is a meeting place for the Orthodox subversives coming up from the valley,' and he walked off.

Soon after, Ali left for another mountain village with his metal wares and a gun. Then Murat came to see Anna.

'Ali sent me, Anna, he lied. 'He wants something out of his drawer in the bedroom. No, stay with the baby, I know exactly where it is. I'll be quick.'

Anna nodded.

Murat knew that the dowry chest was always kept in the bedroom. He lifted the lid, rummaged through and brought out a handkerchief that Anna had painstakingly embroidered with her initials for her wedding day. He folded it and pushed it into his pocket.

'Thank you, Anna,' he called, and ran off.

Murat waited in the square for Ali to return, and then he walked up pretending that he was returning from hunting.

'Just come from hunting?' Ali asked.

'Yes. I went up near the old Orthodox woman's place. I found this on the path just outside her hut,' he proffered the handkerchief to Ali.

'But that's Anna's.'

'Can't be,' Murat said, in mock surprise.

Ali stuffed the handkerchief in his pocket and stormed off.

'Anna!' he shouted, as he walked into their little house.

Anna came running and threw herself into his arms but there were no outstretched arms.

'What's this?' he demanded, and she recoiled at his sharp tone.

'It's my handkerchief,' her forehead wrinkling in confusion.

He stiffened, and fumed off. Anna stood perplexed. Ali went back to the square where Murat waited.

'It's her handkerchief, Murat. I can't believe it. The deceit! I'm heart-broken.'

'Ali. We're expecting an attack tonight. I need you to keep watch on the road coming up from the Orthodox village, Anna's village. They'll probably come from there.'

Ali nodded sullenly.

'If Anna's a traitor, Ali, she'll know about the attack and will return to the safety of her village. If she's innocent, she'll stay. Now take up your post, I've got other duties and then I'll be back in about an hour.'

Murat hurried to Ali's house. Anna opened the door. 'Anna, there's going to be an attack tonight. Ali said you must protect the baby and go to your village. He'll come for you when it's over.'

Murat rushed off before Anna could object. Then he joined Ali behind some rocks that overlooked the road.

'No sign of them yet,' Ali said.

Later, the small form of Anna, cradling her baby, moved along the road to the Orthodox village. Ali stood rigid, numb, his eyes in disbelief. Then a rush of adrenaline and he bolted out from the rocks hollering, 'Anna!'

Anna turned startled, then smiled when she saw Ali.

'Put my son down,' he roared.

She looked confused and put the baby on a small outcrop of grass.

'You betrayed me.' Then the sound of the bullet rang out. Anna fell beside her son.

Ali raced across the distance, tears streaming down his cheeks. 'Take the baby as your son,' he cried to Murat.

'No!' Murat yelled. But the sound of a second bullet had already rung out. Murat choked. Ali was lying on the ground beside Anna, a bullet through his head and the gun still in his hand.

'Ali, not like this. I just wanted my friend back.'

Sultana sighed, the burial was over. One day she would have to tell Anna's son the whole story.

by Helen Collett

Visit by: Herbert Pumblewick

Date: 16th May 2016

On 13th April a call was received by Jeremiah Flintwinch expressing concern about the welfare of the occupants of a neighbouring property. A visit was arranged to gauge social service intervention needs.

I arrived at 3:15pm and after a delay I was met by a young woman who refused to introduce herself. She had a haughty demeanour and she rather reluctantly permitted access after I showed her my credentials. The young woman was well dressed but in a rather eccentric manner, I guessed she was between 18 and 21 years old. Her face and hands seemed clean and she was wearing a good deal of make-up. As I was led through the house in silence, I noted the unkempt and dingy state. On the first floor I was motioned into a dark room. There was a faint light from a table lamp and also from a wood fire burning in a grand stone fireplace. Sitting in an antiquated wheelchair was a woman who I took initially to be aged in her 60s but with further scrutiny, I would put in mid 40s. She was wearing what appeared to be a grey wedding dress complete with garlands of faded flowers.

I asked her whether she was Ms. Havisham. She corrected me by insisted on 'Miss' and would not give her first name. She refused to answer my questions, considering them impudent, instead she extolled the virtues of the young woman she introduced as 'Estella' who stood mutely next to her. She said that my questions could only be answered by her London attorney. When I inadvertently admitted to being single, Miss Havisham increasingly turned the interview towards me. Estella stood proud and disdainful smiling faintly as Miss Havisham repeatedly suggested how beautiful and alluring she was.

In my assessment of capacity I found Miss Havisham of seemingly sound medical condition although she has mobility needs. Her relationship with Estella, a presumed daughter, I found dysfunctional and represented an unhealthy psychological fixation. I recommend an in-depth assessment with a view to relocation of Miss Havisham to a care home where her needs could be more appropriately met. The education received by Estella should be reviewed and a separation of the two may prove beneficial to both women.

The house was unkempt with the main room had not been cleaned for some years, and even the clocks had stopped running. There was evidence of considerable numbers of vermin, particularly over the grand table which I could barely see in the gloom. The open hearth represents a clear fire hazard.

File Notes

Date: 17th July 2016

Report by: Herbert Pumblewick

After the unsatisfactory visit to Miss Havisham at Satis House on 16th May I decided it would be appropriate to make further enquiries about Miss Havisham with her solicitor in London. I visited Mr. Jaggers at his chambers in a ramshackle building close to the Old Bailey. He is of stocky build with black, thinning hair, I found him washing his hands in sweetly scented water. He greeted me with a disdainful air and then rather reluctantly confirmed that he acted as guardian to Estella and attorney to Miss Havisham. He then 'put to me' a rather unlikely sounding story that Estella had been adopted and was actually the daughter of a reformed criminal who worked in Jaggers' own office.

It was at this point that the woman in question brought in coffee. The woman had a withered and tortured look. She took a long look at me and then spoke in anxious whispers to the portly attorney. When she had left Mr. Jaggers turned his questioning on me. He asked me about my family and I was unable to give many details as I had been through a series of care homes as a child. He regretted he had not taken note of my name, and that it was his servant who had alerted him to a similarity to someone she knew. With carefully chosen words he revealed he believed he knew something of my family and had tried to contact me on my 21st birthday, but I could not be found. He said he had had dealings with my father whom I never met. After some legal prevarication and further probing of my background, he came to the point. My mother was in fact Miss Havisham's elder sister, Henrietta, who had died shortly after my birth. The inheritance from the Havisham brewery business had passed to Miss Havisham because I could not be traced. Now that will all change.

So as I am now confirmed as family of the client I can no longer work on this case. I feel it likely that I will move into Satis House, and after settling Miss Havisham into a suitable care home, I hope to marry Estella.

by Rob Stallard

Animal Behaviour

'Right, Sharon, I'm off home.'

'Before you go Sarge, I've just had a distressed woman on the phone complaining about her underwear being stolen from her washing line. I know, if it was me, I wouldn't want the stolen goods back! How do you want me to handle it?'

Sarge, or rather Mike, had been the station Sergeant at Clinton Police Station for over 20 years and had covered most crimes during that time including missing underwear from washing lines.

'Where does she live, Sharon?

'Meadowcroft Road, just off Bentley Park.'

'Well, I have to go past there on my way home so let's have the chitty and I'll call on her. Not much we can do but, at least, I can try and give her some reassurance. In the meantime, ask everyone to keep an eye out for any likely candidates.'

'Here you are, Sarge. It's number 14.'

Mike thanked Sharon and headed off. It took less than ten minutes to arrive at 14 Meadowcroft Road which was a pleasant row of terraced houses, all with carefully groomed front gardens enclosed within rows of picket fences. Mike was able to park right outside.

As he approached the gate, he was greeted by the biggest Alsatian dog he had ever seen and he had seen some monster police Alsatians over the years. The dog rested his front paws on the gate and snarled at Mike. For a moment he was unsure what to do. He wasn't too keen to have an arm ripped off! The dog was wearing a leather collar and a glint of sun highlighted the metal tag hanging from it. He glimpsed the name 'Biff' engraved on the tag.

'OK, Biff, good boy.' Calmly spoke Mike.

Surprisingly, on hearing his name, Biff stopped snarling, took his paws off the gate and wagged his tail in a most delightful manner. Mike spoke quietly to Biff for a few minutes whilst assessing his character. He decided that it might be safe and gingerly started to open the gate. Biff reacted in a friendly way so with added confidence Mike fully opened the gate and started to walk up the path to the front door accompanied by Biff who trotted beside him.

Mike rang the bell and very quickly the door was opened by a young woman who expressed relief at the appearance of a uniformed police sergeant. Mike showed his credentials and was invited in. Biff followed too.

Rebecca Sitch, the owner of the house, showed Mike to the lounge and invited him to take a seat on the sofa.

'Cup of tea or coffee Sergeant?'

'That's very kind of you. Black coffee with no sugar please. By the way, where does your name come from, it doesn't sound like it's from round here.'

'Actually it's from Serbia. Lots of name end in 'ic' or 'itch'. There's quite a few Sitch's in the phone book.'

Whilst Rebecca made the coffee, Mike made himself comfortable on the sofa but felt a little disconcerted when Biff sat beside him. Biff really was a big Alsatian and was actually looking down on Mike.

Rebecca passed a coffee to Mike and sat down.

'Well, Mrs Sitch' Mike began 'I thought I'd pop round to make sure you were OK after your unpleasant experience. Would you like to tell me what happened?'

'There's not much to tell really. I went out to collect my washing from the line and found that my husband's favourite underwear was missing.'

'Do you know Mrs Sitch; I have never come across a case where somebody stole men's underwear!'

'Oh no! It was MY underwear that was stolen. The items just happened to be my husband's favourites.'

Mike coughed a little. 'I see. Perhaps you could give me some descriptions so that if we apprehend the thief we'll have some evidence.'

'There were six pairs of knickers, all identical. Made of sheer material, red with a bow on the front.'

Mike wrote the details down and couldn't get the mental picture from out of his head.

'Mind you, I don't want them back. I dread to imagine why the thief wanted them but I can't think of any reason that isn't hideous.'

Just at that moment, Biff decided to leave his place next to Mike. He walked across the room, taking up much of the space, and cocked his leg against a rather splendid Swiss Cheese plant in the corner. Conversation ceased whilst Biff relieved himself and returned to his place on the sofa overlooking Mike.

'Don't worry Mrs Sitch we'll ensure they are not returned to you if we ever find them. I'll just phone the details through to the station if you don't mind.'

'No, not at all.' Replied Rebecca.

Mike dialled the station and a male voice answered.

'Hi Tom, I'm at 14 Meadowcroft Road dealing with theft from a washing line and I have some details for you to circulate. 6 items of identical sheer red knickers with a black bow on the front belong to Mrs R Sitch.' 'Yes, that's right R Sitch.' Mike hoped the laughter from Tom wasn't audible to Rebecca. He continued, hoping he was covering the sound of the laughter now travelling around the station. 'Actually it's a Serbian name. Apparently many Serbian names end in 'itch' like Djokovic, the Tennis player. I'll speak to you later when I have more information.'

Mike put his phone away quickly and continued his conversation with Rebecca, which was mainly designed to put her mind at rest and to convince her that the thief would be unlikely to return.

'Well I certainly won't be putting any underwear on the line again. It makes me feel sick just thinking about it.'

When Mike was happy that Rebecca had recovered from the shock and had convinced her that the police would do all they could to catch the thief, he finished the coffee, stood up and returned the cup to Rebecca. Biff remained seated on the sofa.

'Thank you for the coffee Mrs Sitch. I'll keep you posted if we make any progress.'

'Thank you Sergeant. I appreciate your help.'

Mike shook hands with Rebecca after which, she opened the front door and he stepped outside.

'Well, cheerio then and, once again, thanks for the coffee.'

'Cheerio.' Replied Rebecca. 'Oh by the way Sergeant, what about your dog?'

by Ian Smith

Sod's Law

Fred Mortimer had a problem. He'd run out of ideas. He lived on his own and had no one with whom he could discuss his predicament, and so he was inclined to have long discussions with his other self, or thin air.

He needed to write a short story with a link to Shakespeare. Which was all very well and good, but Fred wasn't a fan of the Bard, having discovered while still a schoolboy that they weren't on the same wavelength. As he remarked to his parents over roast beef and Yorkshires one Sunday:

"His characters don't talk like us and use odd words like forsooth and methinks."

"Nothing wrong with that," his father had replied, "that's the way they spoke in those days."

"It would be better if someone edited them and brought them up to date," Fred said.

"I disagree," his Mum broke in, chasing a forkful of peas from Dad's allotment round her plate and scattering them onto the tablecloth. "English is a lovely language and you'd take away some of its beauty if you tried to modernise it."

Fred nodded dutifully, but thought it was a waste of time if it took you half an hour to understand what the heck he was getting at.

Fifty years on, and Fred was still of the same opinion; though give him his due, he did rummage round until he found a copy of The Complete Works of Shakespeare in almost pristine condition amongst some of his old schoolbooks; the ones he loved, Treasure Island, Gulliver's Travels, Black Beauty, and Jamaica Inn. The sort you can read again and again even when you've grown up.

He pondered; 'If I were to use quotations from Shakespeare in a short story, would that count as plagiarism? Or, as they are well known, would they be regarded as clichés?'

To be or not to be, that is the question, whether 'tis nobler in the mind to pinch someone else's words, or to write your own pearls of wisdom?

Fred stared at the blank computer screen. "Once more unto the breach" he muttered, hands poised above the keyboard, but it didn't help. Nothing came, no inspiration, no Eureka moment.

His eye was caught by an advert in the local newspaper for a performance of A Midsummer Night's Dream and he booked a ticket straight away. It was the one he vaguely remembered doing for A Levels, which he'd had to re-sit - twice.

He stood in a queue outside the little theatre in the rain until a fight broke out between a couple in front of him. A young man, wearing a baseball cap landed the girl next to him a stinging blow to the side of her head. She retaliated with a swipe of her bag which looked heavy enough to contain a brick, but it missed the offender and gave Fred a glancing blow which caught him off balance so that he fell, knocking himself out on the kerb.

Fireworks went off in his skull; the world went round a couple of times until he found himself standing in a Shakespearean alleyway next to an unkempt ruffian with a handcart full of cabbages and cauliflowers and a barrel of cockles and mussels. Fred picked up a cauliflower and studied it, likening it to a set of brains ready for forensic analysis. He held it aloft. 'Alas, poor Yorick, I knew him well,' he cried dramatically.

"Let's be having you, sunshine," a police officer's voice broke into his soliloquy and he was dragged into a cell by his feet to cool off.

"It was nothing to do with me," he explained.

"That's what they all say", the booking officer said. "The medical officer will be along to have a look at you. Don't leak any blood, I've just mopped that floor."

This reminded Fred and he put up a tentative hand. Yep, there was a whacking great bump on his temple the size of a … an ostrich egg. Well, almost.

The M.O. put a plaster on it and told him to go home, "and pick your friends a bit more carefully in future," he advised.

"But they weren't my friends, I'd never met them before in my life," he protested, "I was queuing to see A Midsummer Night's Dream - doing research for writing a story with Shakespearean connotations."

The doctor was washing his hands at the sink.

"I can help you there," he said, reaching for a towel, "I belong to an amateur dramatics club and I know all his plays backwards."

Fred was not convinced that backward knowledge would be much help, but ill blows the wind that profits nobody, he told himself, and before long he had enough ideas for stories from the M.O. to fill a book. None of them had anything whatsoever to do with the playwright, but there were numerous ways of getting round that little consideration. He was now armed with a folder full of the doctor's memories of saving criminals from the jaws of death, of last minute requests from prisoners who had botched pretended suicide attempts, amputation of limbs at the side of the road after car accidents, and numerous other gory incidents. In fact he now had so many fresh ideas he considered writing a series for the BBC. Life was looking up and he popped round to the pub to have a celebratory drink.

The following day he started piecing together one of the medical officer's memoirs, being careful to change all the names and places. His main character he called Romeo, which, though not original, would do very well under the present circumstances. The Romeo of his story was a somewhat grizzled old Detective Inspector who was shortly due to retire, but before he was presented with a gold carriage clock by the local Chief Constable, he promised himself that he would have the serial-killer who had been terrifying the neighbourhood, under lock and key.

The killer was a bent rabbi who always sliced a pound of flesh from his victims before finishing them off.

Thoroughly wrapped up in his story, Fred typed away at the keyboard all day and when he had finished, was well satisfied with the result. His determination to complete the work meant that he had neglected to read his emails, and he saw the red light was flashing on his telephone answering service. He pressed the switch:

"Hello, Fred. I hope you're OK. You haven't been answering any of my emails. Computer down? Anyway this is just to let you know that it's been decided to scrap the Shakespearean themed story. Everyone else is doing it on BBC radio and there was Midsummer Night's Dream on TV last night. So as it is the centenary of the Battle of Jutland, we've decided to have a naval theme to the story this year. What d'you think of that? Brilliant eh? An excuse to go up to the Firth of Forth and do a bit of research. Might get some fishing in with any luck. See you next Tuesday. Cheers for now, get back to me as soon as you can."

'Sod it,' Fred said, his head in his hands.

by Barbara O. Smith

A Dickens of a Dream

By David Baldock

In my dream, in slumber deep
A man they called Uriah Heep
Proclaimed that he was very 'umble,
Unlike the pompous Mr. Bumble,
Who, in tones so very cruel
Denied a boy a bowl of gruel.
The trembling lad had asked for *more*
And quickly had been shown the door.

It was the best and worst of times,
And Trotty Veck, who heard The Chimes
And met the goblins in the tower
Saw terror in that midnight hour.
On Yarmouth beach I saw a boat
Turned upside down, no more to float,
"Barkis is willin'!" the old man cried
To Peggotty, his future bride.

While o'er in France Madame Defarge,
Her evil stopped by gun's discharge,
Lay lifeless, while the brave Miss Pross
Still lived, but suffered hearing loss.
And then a man named Jarvis Lorry,
Whose countenance was very sorry,
Picked up a Carton he had seen
Fall topless by the guillotine.

The dream then switched, I'm glad to tell,
To cricket down at Dingley Dell,
Where cad and bounder, Alfred Jingle,
Cheered every wicket, every single.
While Pickwick beamed beneath his hat
At ev'ry thunderous 'How's that?'
And Samuel Weller, trusty soul,
Gave out advice on how to bowl!

Once more the scene turned dark again,
A criminal sought by king's men.
Pip stole some pie from off the table,
Magwitch repaid when he was Abel.
A vicious teacher, Wackford Squeers,
Reduced his hapless boys to tears,
But Nickleby, with Smike in tow,
Brought Squeers and all his cohorts low.

I spotted nursemaid Sairey Gamp,
And then a crumbling ruin, damp,
Defying human habitation,
Ideal for Fagin's situation.
A cunning, scheming, shrewd old Jew
Trained lots of boys in what to do
To pilfer handkerchiefs from pockets,
And watches, purses, silver lockets.

An evil-looking villain, Sykes,
The sort no reader ever likes,
Had in his power his one true fancy,
Then murdered in cold-blood poor Nancy.
We briefly looked at Mrs. Todgers',
A boarding house that took in lodgers.
In prison Micawber drained his cup,
Expecting something to turn up.

I saw a pale, thin ledger clerk
In dingy office, almost dark,
His threadbare coat needs cloth to patch it,
You know his name, of course - Bob Cratchit.
His mean old boss, Scrooge, Ebenezer,
A sour-faced heartless sort of geezer,
Begrudged one day, the very least,
Bah! humbug! to the Christmas feast.

But then the dream turned black and chill,
A ghost at Scrooge's window sill,
With message, ominous and clear
That Scrooge just did not want to hear.
For three more spectres in its wake
Made Scrooge in terror scream and quake.
They made him watch, they made him see
Past and Present and Yet-to-be.

The lesson worked, I'm glad to say,
Scrooge was reformed that Christmas day.
By all he had been much despised
But now the townsfolk were surprised
At largesse scattered all around,
And in the Cratchit house the sound
Of Christmas toast raised just for him,
"God bless us all!" cried Tiny Tim.

A salutary lesson, friends,
And just before this poem ends
Let's think how Dickens took a swipe
At pompousness and all that tripe,
Officialdom, hypocrisy,
Ignorance, want and poverty.
He dealt a blow to cruel oppressors
And made life better for his successors.

The dream went on, but I am sure
You really don't want any more
Of names like Snodgrass, Chuzzlewit,
Barnaby Rudge, Tom Tappertit.
Gradgrind, Claypole, Compeyson,
The list goes on and on and on.
These characters are just the pickin's,
So, all together, "What the DICKENS!"

Cast Aside

"It's stuck over my ears. I can't budge it." Elizabeth was tugging at the plaster animal head fixed firmly over her face and scalp, it was not budging an inch.

"I'll fetch Vaseline. I'll be as quick as I can. Stay there until I return." James, in cream shirt, plus-fours and long white socks, dashed out of the dressing room accidentally knocking Margaret into the door frame as he passed and she entered.

"I'm unlikely to go anywhere like this am I?" Elizabeth replied as he disappeared.

"What's happened in here? Is that you in that ass's head dear sister?" Margaret giggled to see her usually confident older sibling looking so vulnerable dressed in a pale pink cotton dress, white ballet pumps and that plaster head. The large ears had been painted and covered in horses hair, the prominent nose was grey at the tip and white card teeth protruded from the mouth. Two blue eyes peeped forlornly through holes under a heavy brow.

"Help me get it off and stop laughing. It's heavy, hot and humid in here. My stage make-up is streaking down my face, I'm going to have to re-apply it when I remove this thing."

"What time are you due on stage?"

"In about ten minutes. I can't go on like this, it's awful. What can I do? I only wanted to see what it was like inside and now it's stuck to me."

"I could go on for you. I've learned all your lines," Margaret smirked and continued to taunt. "Oh dear I'm sure I can see steam coming out of the ass's ears as I made that selfless offer."

A few weeks earlier a similar conversation about acting could be heard at the girls' home, only the response to their request to appear in the local production of 'A Midsummer Night's Dream' was not as positive as they'd hoped. Their mother was sitting in the orangery reading the morning papers, a shaft of sunlight surrounding her delicate features and a waft of Rose Water filling the air. The girls knew she was concerned about the effect the war was having on the country. She had already moved her daughters from the bomb craters of central London to safer rural accommodation and now they seemed to be happily mixing with local people. She had given them more freedom than their father had agreed but was willing to accept the consequences, she could always get her own way when dealing with her husband. The girls approached her with trepidation that morning before delivering their earnest request.

"Mummy, do you remember when we appeared in the pantomime last Christmas?" Elizabeth, four years older than her sister, hesitantly addressed her mother.

"Yes dear of course I do." Their mother looked up at them over the ridge of her dark rimmed spectacles without moving her head or disturbing the newspaper.

"Well the estate workers are staging a production of 'A Midsummer Night's Dream' and we want to be part of it, I mean Margaret and me. We want to act and help with the scenery, costumes that sort of thing," Elizabeth twisted her hands together in nervous anticipation.

"You can have a role Elizabeth but Margaret is too young to be on the stage in that particular production. She can help with the costumes."

"That's not fair," Margaret crossed her arms, pouted and stamped one foot on the stone slabs.

"Actually I have auditioned for the part of Bottom and they accepted. Isn't that wonderful?" Elizabeth excitedly explained while ignoring her sister's teenage tantrum.

"I could have a part too," Margaret sulked. "You're wrong to think that I'm too young. I know I could do it."

"Bottom?" Mother shrieked. "Isn't he a young man who is turned into an ass?"

"Yes Mummy that's right."

"No Elizabeth that is not a suitable role for you. You would be ridiculed, your father would be very unhappy. Think of your social status. No definitely not. If you must be in the play then you will have a genteel, ladylike role."

"But Mummy…"

"No Elizabeth. Now go and tell them you cannot play the part of Bottom. You can be Hermia or Helena, Titania at a pinch, but not Bottom."

Disappointed but loyal and obedient, Elizabeth learned the role of Helena and four weeks later found herself standing in the dressing room in a pretty dress with an ass's head on top of her own. Helena was the only female part remaining once she and Margaret had returned to the players to tell them of their mother's strict instructions. The estate manager and director of the play, James, had no choice but to cast himself as Bottom.

Elizabeth and James enjoyed learning their lines together while Margaret listened attentively. To appease her sister Elizabeth allowed her to be the prompt during the rehearsals. Now, after weeks of practice, Elizabeth's skull was firmly stuck inside the head of an ass and no end of tugging, twisting and writhing would budge it. The director dashed back into the room and applied lubrication.

"Oh James what shall we do? The Vaseline has made no difference. My ear lobes are turning up making it too narrow for the head to be removed, and it hurts," Elizabeth fought back tears of frustration, panic and pain.

"We'll have to break the ass's head, it's only Plaster of Paris stuck onto chicken wire, it will easily fall apart. Of course it will ruin the production if the audience can't see Bottom as an ass but so be it."

"No!" A muffled cry came from the Ass. "We have to have an ass in the play or it won't be authentic."

"I know what to do," Margaret offered. "James, you can play Bottom the man and Elizabeth can play the ass. She's learned all the lines with you, she'll be fine and no-one will know the difference. You'll have to change quickly between scenes."

"But she is Helena and I have no understudy, the whole production is ruined."

"I can play Helena of course," Margaret said gleefully emphasising every word. "I've heard Elizabeth saying the lines over and over. I know them off by heart."

"No!" The ass screamed and a muted groan followed. "Mother will skin me and you too."

Later that evening when the cast took a bow at the end of the show, Elizabeth, still firmly encased in an ass's head, couldn't help a feeling of impending parental wrath. Her mother and father were in the audience and although unseen due to the footlights she knew they would be angry to have witnessed their youngest daughter on stage playing Helena. They would also be wondering where she could be and why Margaret was playing the part set aside for her sister. To her left she could see Margaret proudly and prominently bowing to the audience, grinning mischievously, having achieved her aim to get onto the stage, relishing the applause. To Elizabeth's dismay the young sibling was not trying to hide the fact that she had managed to get her own way.

James, who until now had concealed himself backstage pretending to be inside the ass's head, rushed up to the cast from the wings and his announcement astonished the players.

"The King and Queen are in the audience and want to meet you all! Quickly line up here on stage they're coming up now! Isn't it exciting!" He bounced up and down as though on a sprung mattress.

Elizabeth grimaced but no-one could see her face. She was tired and her shoulders ached, she wanted to get away and smash her way out of the plaster and chicken wire as quickly as possible. She dreaded meeting the royal party while still inside the head of an ass, perhaps they wouldn't recognise her if she didn't speak.

The Queen, in felt hat, feathers and fur, led the King onto the stage and spoke briefly to the players one by one. Elizabeth was squirming inside her heated plaster and wire cage, perhaps she could disguise her voice. The Queen approached her and spoke softly into the ear of the ass. "You're secret is safe with me, I won't reveal your identity to your father but you have some explaining to do later my child. An ass's head is not a very suitable adornment for the future Queen of England."

Elizabeth heaved a huge sigh and looked at her fidgeting sister who had no opportunity to hide her performance from her father behind the head of an ass, nor did she want to. Margaret curtseyed, smiling sweetly with her head on one side, looking cutely angelic, melting hearts as usual.

As the king approached he was smiling broadly and his eyes lit up when he reached Elizabeth. She shook his hand gently, realising then that he had guessed her secret but she was sure when he heard and understood the truth both daughters would be forgiven, in time.

by Sally Hope Johnson

Cryptogram

Solve the cryptogram to reveal some lines written by Mary Pooley. To give you a start, R = P, Z = K and H = V.

R	E	K	Q		A	E	K	Q	O	J	T	W		M		R	E	J	V
P														P		P			

N	Q	L	F	Z		L	C		M	C		A	E	K	Q		T	J	L	O	K	Q	J
				K																			

O	M	H	E	K	Q		C	P	J		U	E	Q	N	O
		V													

Solution on page 91.

52

A Dickens of a Surprise

I'd been amazed to receive an invitation to my employer's Christmas extravaganza. I'd joined a firm of Investment Bankers straight after Cambridge and was learning the ropes from the base up. I was surprised I'd even been noticed.

"Come in Dickensian costume" to a house in Doughty Street, not far from the City. I decided to go as Inspector Bucket, the nearest I could find in the Dickens cast-list to a problem-solving analyst.

It was just before Christmas. The plaque outside proclaimed the building had been Charles Dickens' main London residence. A four-storey Victorian residence, every room was candle-lit and elegantly furnished.

There was already a crowd but everyone else there seemed much older. They were mostly men, dressed as senior figures like the portly Pickwick or cheerful Chuzzlewit. An angular, Scrooge-like figure was dispensing drinks in the hallway and I queued for my noggin. I assumed this was just the party waiter until I heard him addressed as Dr Scroggie and realised he was the firm's Chairman.

For senior staff this was a time to relax and let off steam. Times were hard, the work ethic within the firm was intense: casual chat was almost unknown. I felt ignored, almost invisible, as I slipped from room to room and floor to floor. But the lack of dialogue at least gave me chance to appreciate the fine furniture and Victorian bric-a-brac in the historic building.

I had reached the top floor - the den - and was taking stock of the desk used by Dickens himself - dare I try the chair? - when I heard a crash and moan from the floor below. Someone was in trouble. Quickly I turned and raced back down the stairs.

I was the first into the third-floor boudoir; and quickly spotted the problem. Mr Pickwick was lying as still as a statue, slumped across the chaise longue, his face ashen white. 'Are you alright?' I asked but it was clear he wasn't.

I needed help. I turned and ran down to the floor below. There were two rooms on each floor and both were occupied by party-goers. But before I could decide which one to alert first, I heard the authoritative voice of Dr Scroggie echoing up the stairs. He was the man in overall charge, I had to tell him.

'There's been an accident,' I panted, as I reached the floor below. 'Mr Pickwick has collapsed. He's in one of the rooms on the third floor. We need an ambulance.'

I must have sounded convincing. Scroggie took me at my word, seized the phone in the hall and summoned an ambulance. Then he growled, 'Show me.'

The pair of us climbed steadily back up the stairs as the party carried on around us. I'd shut the boudoir door when I came down, but as we went in there was no sign it had been disturbed. Pickwick still lay slumped along the settee, a knocked-over chair beside him. Scroggie grabbed a mirror from the dressing table and held it to Pickwick's mouth but there was no sign of breathing. 'I think, you know, he's dead.'

I gulped. This went far beyond Christmas festivities. I had never crossed paths with Pickwick but I knew he was the Financial Director. Investment banking was a cut-throat business; no doubt he had his opponents within the firm - but surely no-one would be that desperate.

'When you found him here there was no-one else in the room?' asked Scroggie.

'No-one,' I replied. 'I heard a noise from the floor above and came to investigate.'

Scroggie looked despondent. 'We'll probably need the police before we're finished, but we'll wait to see what the ambulance men tell us. Let's see what we can deduce for ourselves.'

'Shouldn't we ask everyone to stay where they are until the ambulance has come and gone?' I asked.

'Good idea.'

Scroggie went down the stairs and announced in an authoritative manner, 'Ladies and gentlemen, I'm sorry to inform you that our Finance Director has collapsed. The ambulance will be here in a few minutes. Could I ask each of you, please, to remain where you are until they've gone.'

He climbed back up the stairs and into the third-floor boudoir.

'I see you're dressed as Inspector Bucket. Appropriate. So what can you tell me? What's your name, for a start?'

'I'm George Goode, Dr Scroggie; I joined in October.'

I collected my thoughts. 'After you handed me my wine I worked my way steadily upstairs. I met no-one on the top two floors. After I heard the crash, I came down and found Pickwick, then came down one more flight. In both second floor rooms lively conversations were going on.'

Scroggie was following carefully.

'So if we ask them, it should be easy either to identify the person who came up with Pickwick; or else to prove no-one came up from either room on floor two.'

Silence as other options were considered.

'But Dr Scroggie, you were serving drinks in the hallway below. Did you notice anyone going up from there?'

'There was no-one in the last few minutes, George.'

Another pause. I decided to expose my theories.

'There's one other possibility. If there was someone with Pickwick and he heard me coming, he could have hidden here, behind the curtain. Then slipped up to the top floor when I came downstairs.'

'George, you're right. He could still be there.'

'It's alright. While you went down to tell everyone about the ambulance, I slipped upstairs and locked both doors on the top floor. If he is in there he won't go far.'

In the end it was much as we'd surmised. Pickwick had been stabbed by a syringe, doubtless filled with fast-acting poison. His murderer, an investor with radically opposing ideas, was found by the police locked in Dickens' den.

I didn't stay with the firm for long. Perhaps I was too free-thinking and sociable.

Mainly I just preferred Christmas festivities that were non-fatal.

by David Burnell

The ruby nestling
in the folds of black velvet
dictates its setting.

With light and movement
even the smallest diamonds
flirt with our eyes.

The Shrewsbury Tale

I invite you to come with me for a moment.

Imagine yourself in Shrewsbury, an old market town with cobbled streets, overhanging timbered buildings and a bustling close-knit community. Inside The Three Fishes, a drinking palace since 1780, sat three friends. They sat around an old oak table as they have done for years. A fourth chair at the table was vacant and had been for some time. The foursome was now a threesome.

During each revelry, the friends kept the fourth chair vacant ... just in case. And, while they talked and joked, they tried to avert their gaze from the empty chair. The chair once occupied by Paul, a friend who had brought them together, a friend who was kindly, humorous and so, so sociable. Paul ... Paul ... Paul.

Paul was, at the time, just a few miles away. Having rushed in from work, he plumped himself in front of his laptop, turned on his tablet and positioned his two smartphones at the ready.

His Twitter feed was already busy and, since yesterday, had picked up 15 new followers. He needed to look them up, become their followers, add to his tweets, re-tweet and do lots of likes. His tally was now 502 followers.

It was going to be an exciting night.

Paul started to tweet ... 401 followers.

He continued to type.

301 followers.

301 followers? A blip surely?

No, now he just had 115 followers. 75 followers. What on earth was happening?

Down to 43 followers.

21 followers.

Paul swallowed. Was the system crashing? Was Twitter going wrong?

Three followers ... two followers.

Paul stared incredulously at the screen. Just one follower left. A name he did not know. B y e - bye.

'What is going on?' he whispered.

Bye tweeted.

'In years to come,' he read.' No tweets. No Twitter. Nothing.' Paul blinked as Bye faded from the screen.

No Twitter, no tweets, no followers?

His tablet bleeped.

Snapchat ... Snapchat.

Someone was sending him a picture. Many of his Snapchat contacts he had got to know from Twitter .... The image stared at him.

And it was of him.

It could not be.

Paul - an old man. Hollow, gaunt face. Pale, placid, unshaven.

Alone.

Utterly alone.

Paul stared incredulously.

Who? How? *Why* was he getting this?

The image faded ... Faded into nothingness and the tablet went blank. Black.

Paul pressed the switch. The tablet was lifeless. Useless.

What was going on?

Twitter, Snapchat.

His computer beeped.

A Facebook message.

Paul looked at the screen ... It was Karen, but the picture of Karen usually so smiley, showed her sad.' Goodbye,' And with a click, she ended their Facebook friendship. Karen melted from the screen.

'Goodbye,' another message. This from Sally. Sally from somewhere or other.

What on earth was going on?

Why were his virtual friends deserting him?

Paul leant back in his chair and caught sight of himself reflected in the screen. Bleary-eyed, a little gaunt ... but not yet as bad as the image of himself he had seen, and again, sullen faced.

Paul sat, staring.

No Twitter, no Snapchat and those Facebook farewells.

His room was silent.

His life suddenly felt empty. His contacts - his virtual friends - where were they? They had gone. Disconnected. Deserted him.

Paul swallowed.

And sat in silence.

Paul ... Paul ... Paul, what had happened? What had gone wrong.?

'Last orders.'

Several regulars headed to the bar. It was a busy time at The Three Fishes.

And the barman noticed a familiar face. A once regular not been there for quite some time.

'Hello Paul. Long time no see. What you having?'

Paul, who had noticed his friends sitting in their usual place, bought a round. A big generous round. And he carried the tray over and sat in the vacant fourth seat.

Paul smiled. He was back in the real world.

Twitter, Snapchat, Facebook - unknown followers, unknown friends - part of a false, pretend world.

Whatever had happened, the visitations from the ghosts, images - whatever they were - had brought him back ... back to where he belonged.

'Cheers everyone,' he said, with a broad smile. 'And cheers to you too'.

by Neil Somerville

Far from Home

The
river
of my dreams
carries me back
to faces from my past, unchanged by time.
I
awake
and lie there
in the silence.
A gecko crawls across the sun-baked wall.

Agent of the Crown

Her Majesty held out a hand in regal welcome. 'Come, young man, we do not have long. But there is no need for fear.'

I knew not what she meant. It was early 1585. A courtier had appeared and summoned me to Hampton Court. 'Secrecy is of the essence.' Two weeks later I found myself in the Royal Palace.

'I need someone educated,' the Queen pronounced, 'unknown to the world but able to improvise and to communicate. A man who would glory in serving his Sovereign, at home or abroad.'

I gulped. 'Your Majesty, I would be proud to be that man. But my languages are modest. I was taught Latin, the language of priests; and I learned some Spanish. I have no knowledge of diplomacy.'

'My courtiers all think diplomacy is a form of cheating. You will acquire real diplomatic skills as you go. And you will report directly to me. Now, what do you know of Spain?'

A month later I was a Crown agent, jolting in stunned apprehension to Spain.

Sir Francis Walsingham, the Queen's Head of Intelligence, had terrified me with the grisly details of the Inquisition. I resolved I was not going any closer to King Philip of Spain than was necessary. Navarre, in Northeast Spain, on a major coach route, seemed close enough. I had handled stage coaches in Stratford; soon I found employment at the Hispaniola Tavern in Navarre.

At first, when not at work, I kept myself aloof, writing sonnets in my garret as I refined a Basque-accented Spanish. I garbed myself in local clothing and never spoke in my mother tongue. Before long I was seen as native to the area.

But I was not idle. Gradually I shared the company and the gossip of my fellow-workers. From the porter I learned that diplomatic mailbags passed through Navarre en route to Paris and the couriers stayed the night at the Hispaniola. Further research revealed a weekly pattern in each direction.

So what happened, I wondered, to the bags overnight? I befriended a bedroom maid so no-one would question my presence inside the Hispaniola and over time examined every room. But the breakthrough came when one of the regular couriers, whom by now I knew well, asked me to take his pouch to the tavern-keeper while he repaired a broken rein.

I was excited to have a kingly signal in my hands. How I longed to break open the pouch and read their secrets but I managed to resist. I dutifully handed it over to the tavern-keeper and noted that it was put away in a safe in the far wall. What I needed now was access - regular access - to the key.

Then a message reached me from Walsingham. 'Makest thou progress? Else return at once.' Time was not on my side.

To exert leverage on the tavern-keeper I had been looking for ways of exploiting his reputed affair with the cook. For months it had been the talk of the tavern. But this would take too long. Then, on a minor dalliance of my own, the bedroom maid asked me, 'Why mightest our master have a key hidden beneath his bed?'

It was not certain this was a spare key to the safe, but it seemed likely. There was not much else of value in the Hispaniola. But if it was kept hidden and never used, then could it be replaced by another key that looked much the same so the theft remained undetected?

I stood in position to be proffered the diplomatic bag again. The third time I took it in I spotted the key on the desk, waiting to be used. It was brass but not over-elaborate. Where might I find one which looked much like it?

I recalled coming across a locksmith in Navarre. Visiting him again, I spotted keys of a similar type on display. Taking courage, I went in.

'Sire, the mistress of the Hispaniola hast ordered me to purchase her a new lock.'

'Verily, we have locks: peruse our selection.'

I looked and made my choice. 'This will serve her purpose. But she insists her husband never be told.' My eyes hinted at domestic disharmony.

A few days later the tavern-keeper and his wife had to attend a local feast. They would be late home; it was the chance I'd been waiting for. By the time the pair returned, in something of a stupor, the spare safe-key had been swapped with the one I had bought earlier.

At last I was in a position to read the diplomatic traffic.

For some months all went smoothly. By day I welcomed the stage coaches, dealt with the travellers and cared for the horses. By night, twice a week, I sidled into the tavern-keeper's office and inspected the diplomatic mail. And once a week I despatched a summary report to Walsingham and hence the Queen. Oh the joy of once more deploying my mother tongue!

I learned much. I was one of the first to know that the Spanish Admiral, Santa Cruz, had died; and been replaced by the Duke of Medina. And the diplomatic replies told me that the Duke's expertise was as a soldier not a sailor: he had never been to sea in his life.

My report on this aberration waxed eloquent.

A year later I learned that the Spanish fleet was gathering in Cadiz. This information, coupled with the known naval weakness of Medina, allowed Sir Francis Drake to launch an audacious raid on the Spanish fleet at anchor, which set them back a year.

Later I observed the development of plans to combine the Spanish fleet with an army in Holland. I was able to pass on the inside story on the first, disastrous sailing of the Armada in April 1588, when a storm meant the fleet did not even reach the English Channel. Fortunately I could expand the terse descriptions in the raw signals into something full of high drama.

And I warned the Queen in advance of the second sailing in July. England could not complain it was caught unawares.

All this time I knew I was playing a dangerous game; my luck could not last. I had almost been caught in the tavern-keeper's office when the man returned from a late-night liaison with the cook. Now I sensed I was being watched in turn. Fear of the methods of the Inquisition, applied ruthlessly to my tender body, made it hard to sleep.

So it was a relief to receive the command from Walsingham: 'Thy task is completed. Return at once.'

I had made plans for such an instruction. Whenever I put the stage coaches away I always noted any with empty luggage racks, in which I might stow away. Providentially there was one that very night.

Early next morning I was out of Navarre and across the border to France before the tavern-keeper was even awake. But my sudden exit was tantamount to a confession: if caught I would receive no mercy. I discarded the first stage coach and moved on to a second.

I was out of Aquitaine while the search was still underway in Navarre. A week later I had reached Calais and hired a small fishing boat to take me home.

I did not expect a rousing welcome on my return. I knew from the start that my role as an agent of the Queen must be kept low profile. But I did expect recognition from Walsingham and to be told the impact of my many disclosures.

What I had not expected was that others would have acted on my findings without giving them any credit whatsoever.

Sir Francis Drake's raid on Cadiz had, apparently, been on his own initiative. Nothing much had been done, by the forewarned English, to tackle the Armada as it sailed up the Channel. The Armada had moored at Calais to take on board the Dutch soldiers. But Drake's navy blocked their way back and they had to return round the north of Scotland. It was another storm which smashed the Armada, not naval mastery or first-class intelligence.

'At least,' I mused, 'I could publish some raunchy memoirs.'

I had seen a lot in the last three years; and my writing skills had blossomed.

But Walsingham was adamant. 'William, an agent's role is always secret. Nothing must ever be said about your time away.'

Which was the reason that I turned from reports of life and death for my country to writing plays. I could convey some of the affairs of state in a fictional form.

One of my first plays was a light romantic comedy set in Navarre. I had gone forth as an act of love to my Queen but my labour had been largely unrecognised.

'Love's Labour's Lost' was the right title as far as I was concerned.

[Historians can find no trace of William Shakespeare from 1585 to 1592.]

by David Burnell

Shadowland

By Colin Ferguson

Sometimes, with effort, I can call to mind
the days when we had not been introduced,
and I remembered names, once linked with mine,
sweethearts of yesterday, yet now reduced
to shadowland. Was it so long ago?
Has time made once loved features blur and fade;
young smiling faces that I used to know
close up like daisies in the evening shade.
Now I can see one pair of eyes alone,
one pair of lips are all I want to kiss;
hers is the heart my loving wants to own
and all past pleasures fade into a mist.
So farewell shadowland; you are the night,
and all my future beckons in her light.

Apollo's First Report

Apollo knocked on the editor's door. "Come in," said the editor.

"You wanted to see me, Chief?"

"Yes, I've been reading your account of the battle. An excellent piece of descriptive work but something is missing but I can't just put my finger on it."

"Well, I could go back but it will be exactly the same, history doesn't change. What's happened has happened and cannot be altered unless I make it all up or I could watch the film and write an account of that."

"That's it – photographs, lots of pictures. We are living in the 1950's and our readers expect to see as well as read what's happening. Take the paper's head of photography, George Willis, with you."

"George is too old, at seventy-six I don't think he would make the journey back. I know, I'll take Peter Horton the freelance photographer."

The two men travelled back in time and Peter took many photos during the battle. But, on returning they found that all they had was reels of exposed film. For this they could offer no explanation.

"Read all about it – time traveller reporter Apollo's first report direct from the bloody battlefield of Agincourt". Peter Horton purchased a paper, not having yet read Apollo's account of the battle. Then he ran to catch his bus and settled himself on the upper deck, opened his paper and began to read...

"The year is 1415 during the Hundred Years War. Two months prior to the battle, Henry V crossed the channel with 11,000 men. He laid siege to the town of Harfleur in Normandy. After five weeks the town surrendered but Henry had lost over 4000 men to disease and battle casualties. He decided to march his army northeast to Calais and embark for England but the vast French army of 20, 000 stood in his path holding the river crossing.

I'm standing at the side of the battlefield. I can see 1000 yards or so of open ground with a slope running up to a stone wall. Woods stretch beyond the wall and cover both sides of the field. I think the layout of the site will work to the King's advantage preventing large scale manoeuvres. At the moment the vanguard of Henry's army is moving to the top of the slope. It's been a day of heavy rain and large puddles have formed at the bottom of the slope. The first men on the scene have set up camp. Then they dispersed into the woods and began to cut long poles.

Finally, the remainder of Henry's army have arrived and they too fan out and cut poles from the woods. I cannot imagine why they are doing this. But, once the poles were cut the army is ordered to eat and try to sleep. The rain persisted all night and I managed a little sleep huddled under a tree. I awoke, cold and wet to the noise of hammering. I stumbled to the edge of the wood and watched in puzzlement as the men erected three rows of the cut poles across the field, driving them in at 45 degrees. Half way up the pole an 'A' frame support held it rigid and the end was then cut to a sharp point.

Then Henry climbed up on a cart and summoned the men to come close. I moved nearer in order to hear what the King was about to say. He told them that according to Burgundian sources the French were boasting that they would cut off two fingers on the right hand of the English soldiers so that they would never draw a bow string again. A great shout went up as did two fingers. Remember we do this before we release our arrows.

I am certain, as an observer from another time, that the great speech written by William Shakespeare, you know, the one beginning 'This day is call'd the feast of Crispian' would have roused his troops. Unfortunately, Shakespeare was yet to write his speech.

But now the army formed up in three rows behind the three rows of stakes. The biggest and strongest at the rear, shooting high. The next row shot at a lower trajectory and the front row shot horizontally. The long bow of the English archer can pierce the French armour at 250 yards. The French army approached the bottom of the field. The heavy armoured knights milled around in the mud and from their shouts it appeared they were squabbling as to who should lead the charge and of course by now the ground was a quagmire. Eventually, they seemed to sort themselves out, formed a line across the field and set off up the slope followed by their groups of foot soldiers. At first the horses struggled in the mud but finally picked up speed and more French knights pushed into the space behind them. I could see that this was causing a crush so that the front line could not retreat. Unfortunately the French didn't realise the field tapered slightly towards the top causing them to bunch up. Then one archer let off a range finder arrow and as the French line reached the arrow the English archers let out a loud yell and, as a man, stuck two fingers up at the French before unleashing a volley of arrows bringing down horses and riders. The fallen knights floundered and struggled in the mud but the weight of their armour pinned them to the ground.

Then the King ordered a lightning strike and half the front row of archers rushed forward armed with axes and swords. It was not a pretty sight as they set about a massacre of the French soldiers. Any high ranking

Knight still alive was spared and taken prisoner to be held for ransom.

It was obvious to me that the next charge by the French would be hampered by the dead bodies of men and horses littering the ground in front of them. This of course made it easier for the English archers to pick a target. Under foot the mud churned into a bloody mix making it ever more difficult for the horses to gain a foothold on the slippery mess.

As a silent witness I could see the folly of further charges with the horses slipping in the red mud, each charge more disastrous than the previous one.

As dusk fell at the end of the day the French army withdrew from the field leaving Henry the victor.

Now, I'm looking out over mounds of bodies lying in a sea of bloody mud. I can't help thinking that half of French aristocracy has been lost this day. As someone from another time, surveying the French bodies, it is difficult for me to feel joy at the significant battle won by the English. But compared to the French death toll Henry's army lost about four hundred men and for that we should be grateful.

But, my time here is done and I have received my next assignment. I have to admit I'm not sorry to leave this battlefield despite Henry V being victorious. Now, I am off to witness the battle of Trafalgar. I bid you goodbye from the battlefield of Agincourt."

With a jolt Peter Horton realised he had reached his stop. He folded his paper, picked up his briefcase and alighted from the bus. As he walked towards his house he made a mental note to buy a paper next week. He was looking forward to reading Apollo's eyewitness account of the Battle of Trafalgar.

by Gerry Robinson

How to manifest your destiny in just 6 weeks

Dear Cassandra Williamson,

I wanted to drop you a quick note to let you know that your book 'How to manifest your destiny in just 6 weeks' has changed my life!

I'm not usually into this whole hippy dippy, positive thinking business, but I saw your interview on the Martha Martin show when I was feeling poorly one day and stayed home from work (well, I wasn't that poorly, I just couldn't face going into work).

If I'm honest I thought you were a total con artist. Promising people that they could have anything they wanted through positive thinking; who ever heard of such nonsense? But, out of curiosity I looked your book up on Amazon, before I knew it I'd accidentally hit 'order' and it was on its way to me!

Once it arrived I felt obliged to read it, so that it wasn't a total waste of money, then I thought 'Well, what have I got to lose?' and tried some of your manifesting exercises. You said to dream without barriers, that anything was possible, so I decided I wanted to manifest £200,000 to pay off my mortgage and to quit my horrible job for good.

Sounds impossible, right? I thought so too. But I did the exercises every day for six weeks, just like you said. I was terribly disappointed when nothing changed. Then just before week five was up, literally on the last day, BAM! Everything changed. My mortgage is now paid off and I've quit that awful job. My life is pretty much perfect.

You're an inspiration.

Kind regards,

Susan Barnes

"Well, that sounds about perfect." I thought and pressed the 'send' button. My computer made a whooshing sound as the email pinged off into cyber space.

I hoped she'd appreciate my comments about her book. Perhaps she could even use them as a testimonial. I mean, my story is pretty incredible. I'll bet no one else has manifested anything that big.

I'd put in a lot of hard work into my manifesting. Every single day for six weeks I'd done the exercises (well, apart from on weekends). I wrote down my manifesting phrase 50 times: "I manifest £200,000 to pay off my mortgage and quit my job by 30 October 2016." The book said to write it out 50 times, but I did it on my computer so I that could cut and paste it, so much quicker that way.

In the end it turned out to be very easy really, I don't know why more people don't manifest their destinies. Although, at the time I'd been convinced that the universe was conspiring against me, it was almost the end of week five and nothing had changed. But then, just at the final hour, the universe pulled through and I ended up receiving a windfall pay out.

It was almost midnight on the final day of week five, my husband and I had been to a Halloween party down the street. His costume was pretty silly, just a white sheet with some eye holes cut out. My costume however was much better. I was Dorothy from the Wizard of Oz. I'd spent most of the night drinking prosecco and clicking together my sparkly, red shoes, repeating 'There's no place like home.'

Eventually, my husband replied, "All right, I think we'd better get you home then." Such a kill-joy. I grasped onto his arm as we walked home, teetering on the high, red heels. I really don't know how Dorothy walked all the way to Oz in shoes like that.

I hadn't told John about the book or the manifesting, I knew he'd think it was silly, but in my disappointment about it not working I decided that maybe he could help. Perhaps if two people tried to manifest the same thing, we could achieve it in just three weeks.

But, turns out I'd been right all along. He chuckled at the idea when I told him.

"You need to stop trying to find a quick fix for life, Susan. If we work hard, we can have everything we want, but these things take time." He'd told me, patronisingly stroking my arm as we walked down the dimly lit road, cars whizzing past us.

I was furious. How dare he laugh at me? I was working bloody hard to manifest this great life for us, and he was just throwing it back in my face!

In the silence that followed I received a flash of inspiration. I realised that I couldn't just rely on the universe to bring me my destiny all on its own. I had to have a hand in this too, the universe had provided the perfect circumstance, I just needed to give myself a helping hand to achieve my destiny.

I nudged John off the footpath and into the path of the number 11 bus that was hurtling down the road, the same line I took into work every day. There'd been a split second where our eyes met before the bus collided with him. He looked shocked, and surprised.

The life insurance paid out very promptly: my mortgage disappeared, and the universe even threw in an added bonus; a weekly pay out from John's pension. I guess the universe appreciates it when we play a little part in manifesting our destiny too.

Anyway, I'm so thrilled with the results that I'm now considering what I want to manifest next.

by Emma Rose Bell

Dickens Wordsearch

E	B	O	B	C	R	A	T	C	H	I	T	D	D	Y
S	O	T	Q	P	E	L	O	D	E	F	A	R	G	E
Y	E	W	I	U	R	I	A	H	H	E	E	P	O	L
D	M	I	E	N	P	F	V	I	A	P	Z	X	R	E
N	I	R	D	B	Y	E	D	O	R	R	I	T	E	C
E	S	N	W	A	E	T	E	S	D	A	M	P	E	O
Y	S	G	I	F	E	B	I	A	T	S	I	N	P	P
C	H	E	N	C	A	N	E	M	I	R	C	K	I	P
A	A	L	D	E	K	G	A	N	M	J	A	T	C	E
R	V	U	R	P	O	L	I	V	E	R	W	E	K	R
T	I	M	O	R	T	H	E	N	S	Z	B	A	W	F
O	S	D	O	M	B	E	Y	B	O	N	E	M	I	I
N	H	E	D	S	U	A	S	E	Y	I	R	R	C	E
B	A	R	N	A	B	Y	R	U	D	G	E	N	K	L
E	M	I	S	B	L	E	A	K	H	O	U	S	E	D

There are twenty Charles Dickens characters or books hidden in this Wordsearch. Can you find them?

They are listed on page 91.

Homework

It was dark, but there was some light from a feeble street lamp across the road. The light, however little, was important to me. It enabled me to check that my perception of the orientation of the world relative to me, was how I would want it to be: specifically, I was trying to maintain a vertical posture as opposed to a horizontal one. Wrapping both my arms around the bus-stop sign-post did help significantly in that respect. I had been waiting for the bus for about half an hour, getting steadily wetter as the rain soaked through my clothes. In an effort to divert the rain from running down my neck and under my coat collar, I pulled my cap round so that the peak was at the back. The disadvantage of that tactic soon became clear when the rain on my glasses seemed to make my already distorted view of the world even worse.

My sorry state was, I must admit, entirely my own fault. I had decided on a visit to a pub in order to do some research for a story I had planned to write. Getting into conversation with some of the regulars at the pub quite took my mind off the purpose of my visit and I enjoyed the conviviality of the occasion, it being nearly Christmas, rather more than was good for me and my mission to obtain information on the brewer and their products. I was now paying for my lack of self control with my brain experiencing difficulty performing the simplest of tasks with any degree of accuracy. Just as I was about to give up the struggle to remain upright, a car pulled up beside me.

It took a moment or two for me to work out that the car was a police car and that the man getting out of it was a policeman.

"Are you all right sir?" he asked. The words taken at their face value were an enquiry as to my state of health, but the tone said that he was laying a trap for the unwary.

"Oh, hhi'm fi-ine, thang you Orifice." Oops. The brain hasn't been using my mouth for a while, it needs to recalibrate.

"Come on sir, why don't we step into the bus shelter out of the rain. There's a bench you can sit on too."

Now why didn't I think of that?

"You appear to have a broken lens in your glasses and you have a cut on your forehead. Have you been attacked at all sir?"

"No, no. I'm fine." Mouth control is beginning to return.

"How about a lift to the hospital for a check up then?"

I was about to answer him when a feeling of subterranean disturbance began to shake my body and I had a sudden fascination with the officer's beautifully polished shoes. I could not quell the eruption and suddenly the beautiful shiny shoes were hidden under a layer of the object of my evening's research.

"I'm sorry officer, really I am. You should go and get cleaned up, I'll get the bus." Speech was getting easier but I wasn't so sure about standing unaided.

"No sir, I can't leave you here. For one thing, there are no more buses tonight and for another, I have a duty of care. I'm obliged to ensure that you are safe."

I gave in. The driver helped the first officer to get me into their car and they took me to the local A & E department and left me in the care of the triage nurse.

Over the next few days an idea formed in my mind. The evening had not been a total waste of time after all. In a week's time my writing group would reconvene after the Christmas break. Before the break the chairman had suggested that we wrote something that had a connection with Charles Dickens. He also asked us to consider contributing to the anthology that the committee were putting together. I now believed that I could write up that evening's experience and fulfil both tasks in one story.

The writing group's first evening back arrived and about half an hour into the meeting the chairman said, "Walter, would you like to read your story next?"

Feeling a bit smug I said "I just have one story but I believe it fulfils both the requirements you suggested before the break."

I then read my account of that evening, hoping that everyone would be amused. When I had finished reading there were a few indulgent smiles around the table but a lot of puzzled looks too.

"I'm sorry Walter, but how does that link to Dickens?" the chairman asked.

"Oh dear. I forgot to include a vital bit of information. PC Shiny Shoes was actually PC Dickens. I thought that would amuse you but without that information, the story's a bit of a damp squib, isn't it?"

"Never mind, it was a nice try," he said. "and what about the other element you said was in your story, the link with Shakespeare?"

"Shakespeare? Oh no, I thought you said Brakspeare!"

by Walter Jardine

70

The Tempest

Ferdinand could not remember the days or for how long they had been on their journey.

The sky above and the waves below were shimmering in the hue of slate. They looked like lava stones at the sunny harbour of Boscastle with the huge difference that now they balanced on the verge of life or death on the open sea in the middle of the nowhere.

His thoughts drifted away from the storm involuntarily, bringing him back to the time when he stood at the very top of those blackened rocks alone as if he had been a hero with his red dragon resting at his feet and a silver sword in his belt engraved with a prancing lion on both sides, its hilt covered by pure amethyst. Clothed in his dusty garment and trousers made by an inexperienced hand of an unknown woman who existed only in the hidden web of his vivid imagination.

Then, some renewed waves jerked him back to reality again and he frantically tried to strengthen his grip on the railings that were cold and slippery by the unsettled foams of the mud spitting by the wind; the wind, which seemed to be by now perpetual.

The blow swept towards him constantly so he did not need to open his eyes and look at the sprinkled foams so that he knew the special lava colours of the horizon, which was so characteristic of Britain as if it were a different Heaven.

He would have loved it in other circumstances but now his heart was pounding with fear and every attempt was in vain to bury it into his fantasy.

In the stormy gushes of wind and dark blue thundering, only the gunwale separated him and his company from the roaring ocean. The tiny raindrops felt like sharp icicles on the thin fabric of his mariners shirt.

When he set off for this trip with Miranda, Gonzalo - the captain of the ark - and Caliban his cyber dog, the weather had seemed to be peaceful without even a shadow in the sky. Perfect for a little sailing.

"Captain, Ferdinand!" shrilled Miranda's voice from the lower deck.

"Do something! Or we all are going to die!"

"Check the ropes! We must get out of here to dry land!" sounded Ferdinand's voice overwhelmed by the constantly besieging blasts and the waves.

"Stay where you are! I can see something over there."

It might be an island. I will try to steer the ship there."

"Patience, patience. You just need a little patience." said Caliban the cyber dog. Only he could preserve his cool in this situation, as truth, patience and kindness were inherent in his cybernetics nature. He was programmed to serve his masters.

"Bloody storm, it is as if someone has cast a magic spell on our heads. Can you tell me where we are?"

"No, I am not supplied with navigation utilities." said the dog with sympathy.

At this moment the ship jerked back then suddenly stopped and they all fell down on the dirty boards of the deck.

"What is this?"

"Where are we?" asked Ferdinand and Miranda.

"I don't know. I think we have hit a rock."

"Look, there is an island! Come on, let's hurry! Bring the dog!"

"As if I could not walk on my own. Are you trying to stitch me up!" remarked Caliban, expressing his resentment and started to follow the others with wounded self-esteem. The water could not damage his synthetic fur. It was coarse and brownish with some hints of light cream colour.

As soon as they reached the shore the storm ceased as if it had never existed and faint rays of the sunshine started warming up the air.

"I don't believe it. What a suck." Ferdinand collapsed down into the wet silt which shone dull gold like a fruit in a watery painting.

"Does anyone have any idea about where we are? We are all too exhausted to explore the place right now. We should send out the dog to look around until we get ourselves together. We need some rest before we should do anything." he suggested.

"I can only agree." said Miranda.

Ferdinand glimpsed at her brittle beauty as she seemed to be so strong. He gently stroked her thin face smiling at her reassuringly.

"As for me I will look around near to us and try to collect some wood to make a fire. We are going to freeze to death if we spend the whole night here.

"Come on Caliban, let's go" commanded Gonzalo firmly.

"Okay, just patience." said the dog and he run ahead sniffing at the balmy air.

The shore around lay peacefully and innocently in front of wild bushes and lush wood behind. The sea turned to harsh orange colour. The sun above them began to settle down painting the horizon into sad purple-blue with solemn tranquillity.

Gonzalo and the dog disappeared behind the strange vast, brick coloured leaves of the nearby forest. There was no trace of green.

"I hope they will be back soon. This place must be dangerous." Ferdinand thought but said nothing.

They heard natural music. They felt delighted by the soft whispering which was humming into their ears. The isle was full of noises which sounded intriguing, everlasting, even ethereal like the music of the spheres: the bees were buzzing, the wind was playing on its pan flute, the forest and the ocean were dashing by thousands of twangling instruments but they were not hurt. They were even peaceful, swinging them into sweet harmony.

"Oh, wonder! How beautiful this all is! How many goodly creatures live in this peace, I wonder. There must be other living people here apart from us." whispered Miranda.

"Were I in London, I would get some soil samples to an oil company. There must be a huge amount of oil around here. We could do a lot of bargaining of it. It could be used even as fertilizer." Ferdinand said, pointing at the dark-yellow cobble-crumbs of the shore.

"Are you mad? How can you think about business even right now? We might not be able to get off this island at all and you can not think of anything else but trading?"

"A minute ago it was you who was talking exuberantly about the beauties of this place." reminded Ferdinand.

"We still don't know where we are actually. This must be a place that so far nobody had discovered before."

"Yeah, it is true. I have never seen any place like this. We should give it a name and insert it into our Almanac of the Year 2516. Our scholars and physicians would be delighted by the news. We could make this place paradise."

"Oh, Brave New World!" Miranda sighed dreaming turned her head into one direction.

"Softly now, silence. Juno and Ceres whisper seriously. There's something else to do. Hush and be mute, or else our spell is marred."

"Spell? What are you talking about? We might be found by tomorrow and we can be home eating cherry pie and drinking champagne."

"Look! Those trees are alive! They were moving! I am sure I saw them coming closer." Miranda suddenly exclaimed.

At this moment the dog ambushed Ferdinand's shoulders.

"Ugh-ugh-ugh." he said. He sometimes talked in his natural language.

"Gosh, what are you doing? You frightened the hell out of me."

Then Gonzalo stepped out of the shadows of the tree trunks and approached them.

"He-he." he said sarcastically. Don't you remember? Patience. Just patience," and burst out laughing.

"It is not funny at all. Have you found anything? I am hungry and Miranda says she saw the trees moving. We had better find a shelter for the night before we get into trouble. Did you find anything edible?"

The thought of food started Gonzalo's stomach rumbling. All their food had soaked away in the storm.

"I must find some food later. But you would never guess who I met at the top of the hill." he said.

"No. With the porter?"

The dog lay down next to him panting. Purple night sneaked above them with millions of lazily twinkling stars.

Then they all heard the soft humming from the direction of the foliage.

"Not to buy, not to buy. We are not here to sell so not to buy. Ariel, Ariel is our boss and he is so exquisite. Therefore not to buy from us, not to buy. All is free so not to buy."

"Who is there?"

"Just the wind. This is what I talked about. Ariel. Whom I met. The spirit of the island. I have talked to him on the top of the hill and he offered his help."

"Did you meet someone?"

"Who is he? Why is he in the island?"

"What are these voices?"

"He looks dead or alive. He looks like a dead fish. And smells from head to tail. But he is intelligent and knows a great deal of this island. He talked about this planet's place amidst the clusters of galaxy. He talked about prosthetic meal, hyper timing, and embryo criticism. He is a far more advanced being than we are.

He is said to be a journalist in his own planet, he has a map of the whole island and he is able to guide us to discover the place but he is obliged to make notes about our progressing.

He said this place is unique. This is a commonwealth of the New Brave World where all things are executed: there is no envy, no kind of traffic, no name of magistrate, no politics. No letters, covetousness, treason, falsehood and pardon should be known. No riches and poverty and use of service none. None contract, succession, bound of land, vineyard. All women too but innocent and pure, no apparel but natural. No sovereignty, no use of metal, corn."

"Very foul."

"All things in common nature should produce without sweat or

74

endeavour."

"No marrying 'mong his subjects?"

"None. But there is something else too."

"I thought there was. What is that? I don't mind his oddities and his island's but I am cold and very hungry. Lead us to him at once! What are you waiting for?" Miranda said.

"Yes, let's go!" Ferdinand jumped at his foot.

"Are we going?" the dog asked.

Gonzalo shifted from one foot to the other.

"I don't know what to do. The only problem is that this might all not be real. We have to find out what is going on here. Someone may be playing a practical joke on us. I don't know. I fear." he acclaimed reluctantly. He then continued.

"As I walked down from the wood I found this note pinned to the trunk of a tree. It was pinned very near to the edge of the path so that anyone who walks there may notice." he said after a long break and pulled out an old slip of paper from his pocket.

"Come on, read it." Ferdinand said.

"What is in it?"

Miranda also stood up and looked at Gonzalo with impatience.

Gonzalo started to read the note carefully, word by word with a hoarse voice:

"Contestants! You have been chosen as testers of our latest computer game. We transported you four into the game so you are now inside our biggest galactic computer. This is a game. Your task is to get off the island without killing each other. If all of you are alive by the end of the game you are free and we grant you each ten million pounds plus a big prize. If any one of you dies, you have lost. In this case you remain where you are and get nothing. The game has already begun. Good luck. Google"

by Marta Cseh

The Kind Gentleman

It was a real pea-souper, swirling yellow fronds of fog wound around the gas lamps muffling every sound. Samuel Wildblood trudged along, head down, his face obscured by the large woollen scarf wrapped around his lower features.

"Buy a match mister." A thin voice brought him to a sudden halt. He peered through the gloom to make out a ragged girl offering him a box of matches.

He shook his head. "You should be at home girl, not standing out in this freezing fog."

The girl took a step back. "I ain't got no home to go to sir – the streets are my home."

Samuel thought for a moment and then offered her a coin. "I'll take a box. Now go and buy a hot pie and try to find somewhere warm."

He pushed the matches into the pocket of his large coat and continued on his way. The match girl looked at the coin – it would buy her some hot chestnuts from the vender on the corner, at least they would keep her hands warm for a while.

Samuel closed the door of his neat three storey house in a middle-class part of the City, and unwound his muffler. He strode into the sitting room.

"Samuel, dearest, come to the fire, you must be shrammed," his wife Leonara cried helping him divest himself of his coat.

"Indeed I am my dearest." He glanced across the room. "And how do you fare today, Mrs Atwicks?"

Samuel's mother-in-law, Sarah Atwicks, looked up from her corner near the fire. Dressed as always in black just like the dear Queen she would say, dabbing her eyes with a black trimmed handkerchief. All for show thought Samuel, Mr Atwicks had met his maker many years ago but his wife liked to face the world as a poor widow woman. "Middling, Mr Wildblood," she answered.

"What's this?" Leonara took the book of matches from Samuel's pocket as she prepared to hang his coat on the stand in the hall.

"I came upon one of the street urchins, a girl selling matches – skinny little thing – I thought it charitable to purchase the matches."

"Of course dear, so thoughtful of you."

"Will she do?" enquired Mrs Atwicks from her corner.

"Very much so, in fact you shall see for yourself tomorrow. Leonara tells me the last unfortunate left this morning."

Mrs Atwicks sniffed. "I fear it was not a very satisfactory outcome, the gentleman in question appeared somewhat rough in appearance."

Leonara set a drink in front of Samuel. "I do worry sometimes about the young ladies' futures."

"Nonsense Leonara, we are securing them a brighter future," admonished her husband.

"Of course you are right, Mr Wildblood." She seated herself in the chair by the fire and took up her embroidery.

"The girl I met today will be thankful for a warm place to sleep. I will bring her home with me tomorrow and no doubt you will make her feel very welcome, Mrs Atwicks."

"Undoubtedly Mr Wildblood."

The fog lifted overnight to be replaced with an icy blast heralding snow.

"Wrap up warm dearest," advised Leonara handing him his gloves.

Samuel nodded and strode down the steps to the pavement. He gave a cursory glance at the boarded up basement window before setting off at a brisk pace.

After doing disagreeable business with one Bill Sykes and the equally odious Fagin he dined with a few cronies at a chop house. Therefore it was almost dark when Samuel retraced his steps of yesterday. And sure enough, there was the girl. In the light of a gas lamp he could see how mal-nourished she appeared. It would take a few of cook's apple dumplings to put some fat on that poor frame.

It was obvious the girl did not recognise him as she proffered a book of matches.

"You do not remember me?"

"No sir."

"I bought matches from you last evening and advised you to purchase a hot pie."

The girl gave a little smile. "And I did sir, but I bought hot chestnuts, to keep me hands warm," she explained. "But thank you, I doesn't meet many gentlemen as kind as you."

Samuel dismissed her thanks with a wave of his hand and peered up at the darkening sky. "I think we are due for snow – do you have somewhere to shelter?"

"No sir."

"Then it is settled, you will come home with me and my dear wife will look after you."

The girl stared at him, backing away. "Oh no sir, I couldn't do that –

what would your wife say if you brought such a poor specimen as me into your house?"

"She would be overjoyed – she lives for her charitable works – be assured you will be most welcome."

And so the kind gentleman and the little girl made the short journey home.

"Leonara my love, here is the little girl I spoke of." Samuel pushed the girl to the middle of the room. Mrs Atwicks surveyed her from her seat by the fire and sniffed.

"You poor thing," cried Leonara. "You have no coat or gloves, come to the fire and warm your hands."

The girl crept towards the blazing fire making certain to edge away from the strange lady in black. She jumped as that same lady asked. "And what is your name girl?"

"I ain't got no name, mistress."

"Then we shall call you Betsy."

"Another Betsy," whispered Leonara.

"What was that dearest?"

"Nothing, Samuel"

"Now, if you are warmed, Mrs Wildblood will take you to the kitchen and find you some vitals."

Leonara held out her hand. "Come along, dear, you shall have a nice bowl of broth and then I will take you to your room."

Cautiously the girl took Leonara's hand.

As they left the room Samuel called "And Leonara my love, remember to return the keys to me when our little guest is securely settled in her room."

Leonara smiled. "Of course my love, of course."

by Joyce Robinson

Brainstorming with Bill and Chris

At the Eel and Anchor Tavern in Southwark, in the late afternoon.

Chris is sprawling at a table, drinking happily. All at once he becomes aware his friend Bill is standing in front of him.

CHRIS   Why so glum, Bill? Sit down man, a jug of ale will put you to rights.

BILL   It's alright for you. Your Tamburlaine is pulling the crowds in. I spent months writing my last play and now they don't want it. It's a comedy, a good one though I say it myself. But the boss said all that counts is bums on seats and comedies are not in fashion. That's your fault.

CHRIS   Well, I'm sorry you're so down but you can't blame me. The people love blood and violence. You know the theatre's packed at every performance. I'm writing Tamburlaine Part 2 now. The boss can hardly wait for it.

BILL   Pox take it, if all they want is battles and slaughter, I need to find some inspiration for something on that theme.

Tosses back his ale and pulls out a thick volume, which he waves at his friend.

C'mon, Chris, we've discussed this book of chronicles before. Remember that tale of the Scottish king being murdered? D'you reckon it would make a play? It's bloodthirsty enough.

CHRIS   Yeah, there's plenty of killing in there, but y'know, old man, the boss won't take it. Too similar to mine, you see. The audience would boo you and they'd want their money back. Then you'd lose your job altogether.

BILL   Mmm, s'pose so.

He runs his fingers through his hair and flicks through the pages again.

What else is in here? Hey, listen. The story of the old king with three daughters, two nasty and one nice – there could be a lot of drama in that...

CHRIS   Pffft! That'll never get bums on seats!

He drains his jug and beckons for more.

BILL   Beams suddenly. Got it! Something quite different. A fantastical extravaganza – fairy king and queen, magic and enchantments –

CHRIS   severely Bill, have you been eating those red mushrooms again? Fairies! I ask you!

Gulps most of his ale and slams the jug down.

BILL   Mushrooms indeed! You're more than half soaked, you are.

He looks into his empty ale jug and sighs deeply. Chris...

CHRIS   Cadging again? You'll have to get a proper job. Oh well, alright, I can afford it today. Tapster, over here!

They both drink in silence for a while.

BILL   So, this Hollinshed book's no use. But I need inspiration and quickly....hmmm, d'you remember that story in verse about two star-crossed lovers. It was set in Italy, wasn't it? Two warring families, *hic...*

CHRIS   Tha- that'sh just a sho-soppy love story. It won't put bums on seats. *Snigger.*

BILL   *His face lights up.* You're wrong there. It's all coming to me. Family feud – duels –street fights – poison. Lots of blood and a bit of romance and then - tragedy. Yeah! I can write that.

He jumps up, staggers and wends his unsteady way to the door.

CHRIS   You owe me a jug of ale. And if the boss takes a play like that, I'll eat my hat. He sinks his head on his arms and dozes off.

by Elizabeth Berk

80

Shakespeare to the Rescue

Jenny sat down at the kitchen table and decided that life couldn't go on. Well that's not quite right, she thought to herself. Of course life will go on; it's my life that won't go on or rather the life that I'm leading. .At twenty five, her life was getting on but going nowhere. She had had plenty of boyfriends but they always seemed to be self centred or so dull. Why is it, she thought to herself, that I only attract dull men? The revelation swept over her, the reason was because she, herself; led a dull and uninteresting life.

She sat back in the chair. A smile lit up her face. The answer was clear. If she wanted to break out of this spiral of dullness she simply had to become more interesting, which meant doing something interesting. But how did she do that? The smile disappeared. As she sat there her eyes involuntarily scanned the room and alighted on the local newspaper in the magazine rack. Perhaps that contains a clue she thought. What interesting things or people had made the pages of the paper? She picked it out of the rack

The front page featured; complete with photograph, a crash of two vehicles in the centre of the town, so not much help there. As she flicked through the inside pages she spotted an item about a local theatre group. It seemed that the Spelthorpe Players were looking for new members in anticipation of their next production. Being an actress, now that would be interesting. Jenny took the paper over to the telephone and rang the number that it gave. A male voice answered.

'Hello', said Jenny, 'I saw the piece in the local paper that said you were looking for new members. Are you the person I should speak to?

'Yes, I'm the one you want.'

'Well, I've always been interested in acting'. Jenny crossed her fingers as she spoke.

'Right.' said the voice at the other end, 'we are holding auditions on Tuesday evening, do you think you could get along?

'Absolutely,' said Jenny, 'just let me know where at what time, and I'll be there'

'By the way, we are doing Shakespeare, what with the four hundredth anniversary of his death and all that. I take it you are familiar with the works of Bard'.

'Shakespeare? Of course, who isn't?' She hoped the slight hesitation in her voice didn't betray the fact that since being forced to read it at school,

Shakespeare had never been high on her priorities.

Armed with the time and the venue, Jenny turned up to the audition to find that she would be taking part with four other young women. Barry, the young man she had spoken to on the phone, who turned out to be young, tall, good looking with tousled hair, was conducting the auditions. He sat with two other adjudicating members in the front row of the seats of the small theatre, whilst all four performed the chosen piece on the stage. A quick discussion with his colleagues followed, after which Barry talked to the hopeful women one by one. Jenny was the last he spoke to and she didn't need him to tell her that she was the worst.

'I'm sorry Jenny,' he said, 'but I'm afraid that we won't be offering you a part in the play. I know this must be a blow to you seeing how you always wanted to be an actress but if I'm going to be absolutely honest, I don't think acting is really your thing.'

Jenny felt it was time to come clean.

'Let me be honest with you then Barry, I never thought of being an actress until I saw the piece in the paper and I've never been a real Shakespeare fan. The truth is that I became fed up with living such a dull life and it seemed that being involved in acting, offered something more exciting and interesting. I'm sorry to have wasted your time.'

Barry put his hand to his mouth as if he was thinking for a few moments.

'Perhaps I ought to explain Jenny, when we said we were looking for new members we weren't just thinking of actors and actresses. A little amateur dramatic group like ours needs people behind the scenes to help run things'.

'What sort of things?'

'There are jobs like organising the ticket sales; there is sourcing the costumes. There are a hundred and one things that have to be done. You seem to me to be bright and capable of tackling some of these tasks at least.. There is one drawback though; you'd be working alongside me.

Jenny looked up into his dark brown eyes.

'When do we start?'

After five successful shows, the cast had a little end of the run celebration on stage, emptying a few bottles of Prosecco. For Jenny it had been a hectic time but seeing all her hard work help towards such an brilliant result, she had never felt so rewarded in all he life. She discovered talents she never knew she had.

Barry handed her a glass and as he bent over to kiss her, he said, 'You have been terrific.'

Jenny looked up at him, 'I was worried that I would make a comedy of errors so I just hope it was - As you like it.'

Barry smiled and gave her a hug. 'I see you've been swatting up on your Shakespeare plays.

'I have,' said Jenny, snuggling in the comfort of his embrace, 'and the one that suits the way I feel right now is -. All's well that ends well.'

by Dick Sawdon Smith

Sunset In Oxford

Orange sun cradled
by the limbs of two trees
loath to let go.

The light on the river
against the black ripples -
embers of fire.

Oars dip the surface.
A line of eight shadows
add music to silence.

O. Disser–Poyntment

Literary Agent

Rowling Mews,
London.
15th March 1591

Dear Mr Shakespeare,

I refer to the recent receipt in this agency of your various (unsolicited) manuscripts for our consideration. I regret to inform you that on this occasion your work does not meet the exacting standard we require of our authors. As Deidre my assistant always tells me, some are born great, some achieve greatness and others have greatness thrust upon them; unfortunately sir, you have evaded all three.

I hope this rejection does not come as too much of a disappointment (although surely it can hardly be a surprise). Each year we receive several thousand manuscripts (unsolicited) but we take on just two or three new writers; you can see what you are up against. I find your work is flawed on numerous counts and by way of kindly guidance I draw your attention to but a few of these below.

On a general point you have an annoying habit of inventing words and phrases; in fact, considerably more than I could shake a stick at. I must ask, is our current repertoire of words insufficient for you, or do you lack an awareness of their existence? Just one example is the word apostrophe, with your suggested examples of its usage. I cant help feeling that this will lead to much confusion in the future in our childrens education, let alone their parents. And how our vegetable sellers will struggle with tomatoes and potatoes. What's more if all children made up their own words who would mark their spelling tests? I urge you to desist with this unnecessary complication.

Your work also suffers too often from much indecision. An example resides in the sonnet you submitted which begins "Shall I compare thee to a summers day". Quite frankly if you the writer is unsure, why should the reader be bothered. My advice is if you are in doubt leave it out. In any event the sonnet works adequately without the first line; simple as.

Indecision also manifests itself in your submission "Hamlet" with the Prince bemoaning to himself "To be or not to be, that is the question". He then goes on interminably. Although he eventually gets to the point you should cut to the chase and remove the waffle (a little word of my own). Thus, an improvement would be "To be or not to be, that is the question.

The answer is, to be, so get over it". Do you see how that works so much better?

I note also rather a lot of defeatism in your writing; considerably more than our readers would enjoy. One example of many is in the sonnet commencing "Farewell, thou art too dear for my possessing". To be blunt Mr Shakespeare, nobody likes a loser. I suggest you replace the first line with "Cheerio, you weren't that special anyway."

I must advise you that plot is of the essence in good storytelling. However, resorting to heart tugging is not a good plot method, its a cheap trick. In your Romeo and Juliet for example, one lover dies, then the other lover dies, then the first lover comes to life again (or is it the other way round). Play-goers would depart the theatre broken hearted, perhaps never to return. You should aim to have them leaving cheered-up. I suggest you make an amendment as follows; one lover dies, then the other lover dies, then the first lover comes to life again and then the second lover also comes to life again, perhaps with a loud and cheery "only joking".

Apart from the flaw noted above your Romeo and Juliet has an adequate story line; two gangs of young bloods battling a turf war on the streets, with a girl involved. Have you considered setting it to music?

It is impossible for me to overstress the importance of titles. It is the title that first grabs the attention of an audience. Consider therefore your title "Much Ado About Nothing". Ask yourself William (can I presume a first name familiarity), who wants to waste a whole evening at the theatre watching a play about nothing. Well, not me for starters. Playgoers should feel they have been yanked by the cod piece into the theatre and then drizzled with drama. So much more gripping than "Much Ado About Nothing" therefore would be "Terrible Fuss About Something". Do you see the difference; did you just feel a tug on your cod piece?

In a similar vein I refer to your title "Alls Well that Ends Well". Where is the mystery in that! Theatre goers will be saying to themselves 'lets not bother with that one, it pans out OK in the end.' How about changing the title to something like, "Alls Well, but Its Not Looking Good".

Just as titles are important so too are the names you choose for your characters. I have in mind here your character Macbeth. A far too innocent sounding name methinks. Greater impact would be achieved with something more sinister; Mac-the-knife-Beth for example. Well 'ard, or what!

And now to A Midsummer Nights Dream. Fairies and stuff. Sorry William, but what were you on? I am left wondering if that "funny tobacco" has now reached Stratford-upon-Avon?

I could go on and on, just as you do, but to conclude I feel that if you act on my helpful advice you may secure some modest success, although I should warn that we literary agents are rarely wrong. If you insist on persevering despite your many shortcomings I understand some writers are now resorting to the use of home-printing presses for so called self publishing. Be warned William, at the end of that apparent rainbow awaits an overflowing midden.

I shall return your manuscripts by carriage immediately.

Sincerely Yours,

O. Disser-Poyntment.

ps Have you considered joining a Writers' Circle?

by Les Williams

Letter Drop

The letters in each of the columns need to be entered again into the squares immediately below but not necessarily in the same order.

By placing the letters in the right places you will find a question Nora Joyce asked her husband James

Solution on page 91.

Merry Christmas, Rupert

Rupert sat on his bed, shoulders slumped forward disconsolately, his suitcase beside him, half unpacked. It was very kind of his grandparents to pick him up at the end of his first term at his new school, but Christmas wouldn't be the same without his parents. It was hard for a seven-year-old to understand but, as Nana had tried to explain to him,

"It's not mummy and daddy's fault they can't be with you at Christmas, darling. Daddy has a very important conference to attend in the Middle East. I'm sure they would much rather be with you but, sometimes, grown-ups have to do things they don't want to."

He finished unpacking, then went downstairs for dinner. Nana kept up the kind of cheery, one sided conversation that Nanas are good at and Gramps occasionally grunted a reply when spoken to. It's not that he was a grumpy person, it's just that he didn't hear very well and his hearing aid was often on the blink, so he found it difficult to engage in conversation.

After dinner and a silent game of dominoes with Gramps, which Rupert found suspiciously easy to win, it was time for bed. Back in his room he lay in his bed, trying to get to sleep when there was a sudden flash of light. He sat up and switched on his bedside light. There, in the corner of the room, stood a strange looking man. He was dressed like a fairy but he didn't look right.

"Sorry 'bout the flash," he said. "Didn't mean to scare yer. It's dis new 'appearing' techy stuff – but I'll get used to it."

"Who are you?" Rupert gasped.

"I'm your fairy godfarver, innit! Me name's Ron!" he replied in a rather deep un-fairy-like voice.

"Don't be silly!" Rupert scoffed. "There aren't such things. Only fairy godmothers. And anyway, you don't speak like a fairy and you couldn't sit on top of a Christmas tree, you're much too big. And I bet those wings don't work, they're too small for you. And Ron's a silly name for a fairy, it should be Tinkerbell or something!"

"I'll make a note of yer complaints and report 'em when I get back. We take customer service very seriously," Ron said as if reciting a rule. "But, like it or not, Ron's me name. And yer right, the wings aren't real, I borrered 'em from our toy stores so I look more like a fairy. Yer see, dis time o' year we're a bit short staffed wiv everybody preparin' for the big deliv'ry night, so I 'ave to 'elp out wiv social visits. I'm a sort of 'supply-godmother', you know, like when you 'ave a supply-teacher at school."

"I don't know what a supply-teacher is but you don't seem very good at being a fairy."

"That's 'cos, really, me job's lookin' after the reindeer and trainin' up the young ones. They 'ave to be taught 'ow to fly, y'know. I only do this fairy lark in emergencies."

"Looking after six reindeers can't be a proper job."

"Six reindeer? You don't believe all dat rubbish do yer? Dere's fahsands of 'em. One Santa and one sleigh couldn't cover the 'ole world in one night on their own! Nah, we put that story round so we got a bit o' magic, innit?" he chuckled.

"So Santa isn't real?" Rupert looked shocked.

"Course 'e's real. 'E's in charge but 'e 'as a lot of 'elp, an' I'm one of 'is 'elpers"

"So why are you here? Are you going to bring mummy and daddy home for Christmas?"

"Nah. I can't bring 'em 'ome – fairies aren't allowed to talk to grown ups. I was on duty and me Sad-Child-Alarm went off so I 'ave to answer it. I'm s'posed to take yer on a trip to cheer you up."

"Where to? Can you fly? Can you make me fly?"

"Nah, we don't do all that Snowman stuff now. We're all hi-tech. We go frough de fourf dimension!"

"What's that?"

"Well, I don't really understand it, but apparently it's summink to do wiv bendin' the space-time con-tin-u-um." He nodded his head in rhythm with the syllables to help him get it right. "That way, we can go straight to where-ever yer wanna go – in a flash. Well, not lit'rally a flash, I wasn't s'posed to do that when I came 'ere. Fact is, I was s'posed to be invisible until I got used to the place and decided when it was OK to be visible. But, no 'arm done, innit?"

Rupert laughed. He was warming to this rather odd fairy.

"Where do you think we should go?" asked Rupert.

"Well, we could go to the 'North Pole'." Ron made speech mark signs in the air with his fingers as he said 'North Pole', and grinned. "to see Santa's elves packing parcels into 'the sleigh'." He did the speech marks sign again. "But you've probably seen all that in the movies. You know none o' that's real don'cher. Sant's grotto is another part of the fairy tale. We've got massive secret warehouses and sleigh teams all over the world. Makes Amazon look like a corner shop. They're even talkin' about doin' away with the sleighs 'n' reindeer 'n' replacin' 'em wiv drones. Er... I 'ope I'm not spoiling the magic for yer, but I never liked lyin' ter kids."

"No, you're not spoiling anything, but it would be sad if they got rid of the sleighs. I guessed there must be lots of Santas, though, 'cos you see them in all the big shops and I often wondered how on earth one sleigh could whiz round delivering to children all over the world."

"There is only one Santa. 'e's in charge of everyfin' but there's so many people in the world now that 'e can't do it all by 'is-self. 'e 'as deputies everywhere but 'e likes to keep it secret – to keep the magic of the idea of one sleigh goin' round the world deliverin' to all the children in one night."

"I understand, Ron, and I still think it's magical, but I won't tell my parents, or Nana and Gramps, 'cos having one Santa and one sleigh is a nice lie. It would spoil things if they found out that I know the truth. And you might get into trouble for telling me all this."

"Good on yer, lad. Like I said, I don't like lyin' ter kids."

Ron became more business-like.

"Now, what I was goin' ter suggest was we take a look at what yer parents are doin', see if they are enjoyin' 'emselves in Dubai – that's where they are, did you know?"

"I knew they were out east but not exactly where. I'd like to see what it's like there. Must be strange for them to be in a hot place at Christmas."

"It ain't that 'ot this time o' year but it's warm enough for sun bavin'. Shall we go then?"

"Yes please! What do I do?"

"Just stand next to me."

He took what looked like a magic wand from a short scabbard on his belt and held it over their heads.

"One adult and one child to Dubai, please," Ron intoned.

Rupert giggled. "You sound like you're buying tickets for a train."

"In a way I am. Shush, don't talk to me f'r a minute, I 'ave to concentrate."

Rupert stood quietly. Then he was surrounded by a total blackness. He couldn't see Ron. He looked down and found that he couldn't even see his own body! A sudden moment of panic gripped him but the light started to return, and he could see himself and Ron again.

"Where are we?" he whispered.

"It's OK, you don' 'ave to whisper," Ron replied. Nobody can 'ear us, or see us."

Rupert realised that they were floating high in a bedroom. As everything came into focus he also realised that the two people in the room were his parents, getting ready for bed.

"They're going to bed early!" Rupert said.

"Nah, it's nearly midnight 'ere," Ron replied.

"You have a good day, darling?" Rupert's father asked.

"Oh John, I had a lovely day, but I couldn't help feeling all the time that they were just trying to keep me happy so that I wouldn't bother you with my concerns about Rupert and Christmas and all that."

"I expect you're right. They're probably trying to keep us both happy to compensate for ruining our Christmas."

John padded round the bed in bare feet to where his wife was sitting. Sitting on the bed beside her, he put his arm around her shoulder.

"Sam, sweetheart, I know you were looking forward to getting him back home from school and seeing his face when he opens his presents on Christmas morning – so was I! But this conference is really important and, really, we're only delaying Christmas, we won't miss it altogether. And your mum will make sure Rupert enjoys himself on Christmas day, even if we aren't there."

Sam's mood seemed to brighten a little as she remembered something.

"Oh John, I nearly forgot, I bought Rupert an extra present this afternoon to help make up for us not…"

"Don't tell me what it is," John interrupted. "I want to enjoy the surprise with him, when he opens it."

Rupert turned away from watching his parents, a tear forming in his eye.

"Let's go home, Ron," he said quietly.

Ron nodded but said nothing. He held the wand over them and went through the ritual that would get Rupert home. Back in Rupert's bedroom, Ron was delighted with himself.

"I got you back 'ere at exactly the same time as we left. No one will ever know you went! Aw… you're quiet. Wossup?"

"It's not easy being a grown up is it?"

"Life ain't easy, however old you are. I'm nearly 800 years old an' I'm still learnin', innit?"

Rupert couldn't help it, he had to laugh.

"You say 'innit' in all the wrong places Ron," he giggled, "but I like it… innit."

They both laughed.

Ron tucked Rupert into his bed.

"Thank you for taking me to see them, Ron. Now, I won't be sad on Christmas day," he said quietly. I'll be thinking of mummy and daddy and I'm sure they will be thinking of me. Tomorrow, I'm going ask Nana to help me choose presents for them, to make up for them missing Christmas."

"You're a good lad. Glad I was able to 'elp. Time for you to get some sleep, an' I'd best be gettin' 'ome meself. Merry Christmas, Rupert."

Without a sound, Ron just 'popped' out of existence.

by Walter Jardine

PUZZLE SOLUTIONS

Shakespeare Wordsearch

Alonso	Antony	Bottom	Capulet
Cleopatra	Cressida	Desdemona	Falstaff
Hamlet	Horatio	Juliet	Macbeth
Othello	Portia	Puck	Romeo
Shylock	Titania	Troilus	Yorick

Dickens Wordsearch

Barnaby Rudge	Bleak House	Bob Cratchit	Copperfield
Defarge	Dombey	Dorrit	Ebenezer
Edwin Drood	Fagin	Hard Times	Micawber
Miss Haversham	Nickleby	Oliver	Pickwick
Pip	Sydney Carton	Tiny Tim	Uriah Heep

Sudoku

O	G	E	T	N	L	U	I	K
U	L	T	E	K	I	O	N	G
K	N	I	U	O	G	L	T	E
L	K	O	G	T	U	I	E	N
I	U	G	O	E	N	T	K	L
E	T	N	I	L	K	G	U	O
G	I	K	N	U	O	E	L	T
N	E	U	L	G	T	K	O	I
T	O	L	K	I	E	N	G	U

Cryptogram

Pour yourself a poem.
Drink it at your leisure.
Savour the words.

Letter Drop

Why don't you write books people can read?